The

North Hollywood

Detective Club

In

The Case of the Hollywood Art Heist

Mike Mains

Chapter 1

"You killed him, didn't you?"

No sooner had the words left his mouth, than Jeffrey Jones regretted saying them. The man standing before him lowered his chin and glowered at Jeffrey under his eyebrows. Without a word, he went to the front door and locked it. Now there was nowhere to run.

Jeffrey tensed and took a step back. The man turned to face him, his breathing slow and deliberate, drops of sweat glistening on his forehead. He stared at the boy and rolled up his sleeves.

"Yes, I killed him," he said. "And now I'm going to kill you."

Jeffrey stared at the man, wild-eyed, and braced for his attack. The deadly tale of mystery and suspense that he and his friends had stumbled upon was now going to end....

Six Weeks Earlier

"It was a daylight robbery. If I had been home, I would have been killed."

Mr. Kingman's admission brought gasps from his eighth grade math class at St. Mary's Middle School, followed by a chorus of voices: "For real? What happened? Who robbed you?"

Mr. K. was a short man, shorter than many of his students, but he stood tall before them. "I don't know who it was. It was actually a burglary. Somebody smashed my window and broke into my apartment while I was here at school on Monday."

"What did they steal?" a boy asked.

"They stole my computer – my laptop – and they ..." Mr. K.'s voice broke and he fought to steady it. "They stole my stamp collection." He pulled a handkerchief from his pocket and dabbed the inside corner of his eye. "My grandfather gave me those stamps."

A hush fell over the room.

"Are you okay, Mr. Kingman?" a girl asked.

Mr. K. nodded, pocketed his handkerchief, and cleared his throat. In his mind's eye he saw the broken glass strewn across his living room floor, the blood smeared across the table where his laptop had been. He had stepped gingerly over the shards of glass and then broke down in tears when he discovered that his prized collection of rare stamps was missing.

He opened his mouth to speak, choked up, and began again. "I'm okay. Thank God I wasn't home when it happened. I honestly believe they would have killed me."

The class sat frozen.

From the middle of the room, a stocky boy in owl-shaped glasses raised his hand. "Mr. Kingman," said Jeffrey, "what did the police say?"

A chuckle rippled through the class. Jeffrey felt the eyes of his classmates turning his way. He kept his gaze fixed firmly on the teacher in front of him and pretended not to notice.

Mr. Kingman took a seat behind his desk. "I should have known you would be interested, Jeffrey. The police did a thorough investigation."

"Police?" sneered Brian McHugh, the biggest and loudest boy in the school. "What do you want to know about the police for, Jones?"

The words hit Jeffrey like a slap in the face. He twisted around in his seat to face Brian, who sat one aisle to his right and two seats behind him. The old wooden school desk creaked under Jeffrey's weight. "I want to know if they found any clues."

"Clues?" Brian laughed out loud, followed by several students.

Jeffrey blinked behind his glasses. He was used to being laughed at. He turned back to face Mr. Kingman.

Brian swung his arm in a wide arc and addressed the class: "Detective Jones wants to know if the police found any clues!"

Laughter rocked the classroom.

Jeffrey felt his neck burning. He kept his eyes on the teacher in front of him.

Sitting two seats behind Jeffrey, and directly across from Brian, Pablo Reyes wasn't laughing. He sat up straight, gripped the side of his desk, and glared at Brian.

Mr. K. shook his head. "There were no arrests, Jeffrey, if that's what you mean. Whoever did it caught a nasty cut when they broke my window. There was blood everywhere. The police said it was either a drug addict, who needed money for his fix, or a gang member, but they weren't really much help. I asked them what the chances were that they'd be able to recover my property, and they said, 'Slim to none.' Typical."

"Would it be possible to look at the crime scene?" Jeffrey asked.

"Crime scene!" Brian almost fell out of his desk. "You think you're some kind of detective now, Jones?"

"Leave him alone," said Pablo.

Brian swung around in his seat and glowered at Pablo. He was bigger than Pablo overall, with meaty hands, a wide face, and a neck that was so thick he appeared not to have any neck at all. But Pablo was muscular and fast, and the only boy in school who matched Brian in height.

The two boys stared at each other. They had been rivals since the third grade. Brian had the upper hand in football, Pablo in soccer and basketball. Baseball was a draw. Brian hated Jeffrey, because he was Pablo's friend, and because Jeffrey was smart, something Brian was not. For Pablo, Brian reminded him of something his father had often told him: "There are a lot of dumb people in the world, and most of them are too dumb to know they're dumb."

Mr. Kingman stood up and stepped around his desk. "I have to side with Brian on this one. I know you're a smart kid, Jeffrey, but do you really think you know more than the police?"

"That's hard to say without doing an investigation," Jeffrey answered.

"Investigation?" Brian was beside himself. "Jones, are you crazy?"

Pablo's face hardened. "I said leave him alone."

"What are you going to do about it, Reyes?"

Mr. K. took a step forward. "That's enough, guys!"

Pablo appealed to the teacher. "Maybe Jeffrey can help, Mr. Kingman."

Brian snorted. "Maybe Jeffrey's insane."

"Maybe you should shut up."

"Maybe we should settle this outside." Brian pushed off from his desk and stood up.

Mr. Kingman stepped hurriedly down the aisle and planted himself between their desks. "I said that's enough! Sit down, Brian."

Brian hesitated.

"I said sit down."

The glowering boy sat down. He and Pablo stared at each other for a moment, then both of them looked down silently at their desks. It wasn't the first time they'd been close to a fight.

"Look, Jeffrey," said Mr. K., "I know you're good with mysteries, and puzzles, and whatnot, but this is a real crime."

"I know it's a real crime."

"Then let's get serious. This isn't Lois Bell's missing cat we're talking about here."

The class laughed.

Jeffrey blushed a deep red and squirmed in his seat. Mrs. Bell was the school's art teacher. Last fall, her cat, Water Color, had given birth to six baby kittens, and Mrs. Bell turned frantic when one of the newborns disappeared. Flyers went up, search parties combed the neighborhood, and even a bona fide pet detective was called in. But it was Jeffrey who solved the mystery.

He had reasoned that a newborn kitten couldn't wander off very far on its own, and since the only ones who knew about the kitten's birth were Mrs. Bell's immediate neighbors, the missing feline had to be with one of them.

Sure enough, the five-year-old daughter of Mrs. Bell's next-door neighbor had visited just after the kittens were born and had inadvertently brought the missing kitten home when it crawled into her backpack.

The poor kitten was near death when they found it, but Jeffrey's quick thinking had saved its life. He made the school newspaper for that one.

The classroom laughter encouraged Mr. Kingman. He rubbed his hands together and stepped closer to Jeffrey. "Or a case of sour milk!"

The class laughed again, louder this time, and Jeffrey sunk lower in his seat.

Last winter, on the first day back from Christmas break, the lunchtime cafeteria had been met with howls of, "My milk stinks!"

Jeffrey investigated and deduced that old Mr. Flanagan, the school janitor, was responsible. Mr. Flanagan, who was known to sneak a nip from a bottle now and then, was upset over a recent suspension, and had unplugged the kitchen refrigerators at the start of Christmas break, and then plugged them back in just before the students returned, causing the milk to go bad.

The old man confessed when confronted and Jeffrey had solved another case. Mr. Flanagan was fired and the headline in the school paper read: Sour Grapes Over Suspension Leads to Sour Milk. Under Jeffrey's picture, the caption read: Student Solves Case of Stinky Milk.

Smiling now, Mr. Kingman said, "Or toilets that explode!"

The class roared with laughter.

Jeffrey covered his face and slunk down in his desk as low as he could go.

Last April Fool's Day, someone had rigged the toilets in the student restrooms to explode in a gusher of water six feet high at every flush. That was a case that Jeffrey had not solved, but only because he wasn't allowed to investigate. Instead, the school was closed for a day, plumbers were called in, and the headline in the school paper simply said: Flush At Your Own Risk.

Jeffrey never told anyone, but he long suspected that Brian was the culprit behind the prank. He turned to him now and saw Brian staring back at him, his face redder than Jeffrey's and his ears flared out from his head like a pair of angry stop signs.

Mr. Kingman threw up his hands. "Look, Jeffrey, if you want to come by on Saturday morning, you're welcome to look at the 'crime scene.' But don't get your hopes up. I seriously doubt that you'll find anything that the police haven't already uncovered. I mean, let's be reasonable. They're the police. They have crime scene professionals. You still have two weeks to go before you graduate from the eighth grade."

Laughter bounced off the walls. The bell rang. Brian whooped and hopped out of his seat, followed by other kids. Pablo rose sullenly.

Jeffrey remained in his seat and stared down at the floor, wishing he could disappear. Brian walked past him. "Crime scene." He shook his head and laughed. "Jones, you're crazy!"

Chapter 2

Saturday morning couldn't come faster for Jeffrey and Pablo. As they pedaled their bikes to Mr. Kingman's neighborhood, Jeffrey shook his head and said, "It doesn't make any sense. The police told Mr. Kingman that the thief was either a drug addict or a gang member, but why would a drug addict or a gang member steal a stamp collection?"

"They could sell the laptop for money," Pablo said. "But a gang member wouldn't know a stamp collection from a bag of rocks."

"Right, so why take it? You're thinking like a detective, Pablo. There's something funny about this whole case and I wonder if there's more to it than Mr. Kingman told us."

They found Mr. Kingman's apartment building on a busy street in North Hollywood. As they glided in on their bikes, a grey sedan passed them and the faces of three young children peered out at them from the back seat with questioning eyes. On the sidewalk, a couple in matching shorts and T-shirts jogged past, followed by a young mother pushing a stroller. Giddy children dashed across the lawn of a neighboring building, while their mothers gossiped. An elderly man walked his schnauzer dog.

Mr. Kingman met them in front of his building with a smile. "Well, if it isn't Sherlock Holmes and Dr. Watson to the rescue."

Jeffrey and Pablo climbed off their bikes and looked at him blankly.

"That's a little joke," said Mr. K.

The boys looked at each other and then back at their teacher.

"I said it was little."

Mr. K. was dressed in khaki shorts and a white T-shirt. His legs poked out of the shorts like a pair of pale toothpicks. He looked funny to the boys who were used to seeing him in a suit and tie. "Welcome to my humble abode," he said. "The police say the thief jumped this fence." He unlocked a six-foot-high iron gate that surrounded the apartment building. "Or he slipped in while a tenant was coming or going."

"Is this gate normally locked?" Jeffrey asked.

"All the time." Mr. K. held the gate open and the boys followed him through, walking their bicycles.

Inside the security gate, the boys locked their bikes to a metal railing. Pablo knelt to tie his shoe. Jeffrey knelt next to him, pretending to tie his own shoe, and whispered to his friend: "Drug addicts are jittery and suspicious. And gang members can be obvious, too. A tenant who lived here would never let someone like that slip inside while they were coming or going. And look at all those people on the street and on the sidewalk. If anyone suspicious jumped this fence in the daytime, somebody would have noticed and called the police."

Pablo nodded and whispered back, "Now you're thinking like a detective."

Mr. K. led them to the front door of the apartment building and unlocked it.

Jeffrey stopped. "How did the thief get past this door?"

Mr. K. shrugged. "The police say he could have slipped in with a tenant, the same as the gate out front. Or maybe the door was unlocked or propped open. It is sometimes, when someone is expecting a package or a delivery. Or maybe he picked the lock. I guess I shouldn't say 'he'. I mean, it could be a female thief, right? Although somehow I doubt it."

He held the door open and the boys followed him inside to a large courtyard. Two rows of metal mailboxes, one on top of the other, lined one of the walls. Trees and shrubbery decorated the area. Water gurgled from a fountain. Jeffrey studied everything.

"Up these stairs, men." Mr. K. led them to a stairwell and started up. The boys followed, a few feet behind. Jeffrey whispered, "If you were a drug addict, would you come up these stairs to rob an apartment?"

Pablo shook his head. "I'd take the first apartment downstairs. The closest one."

Jeffrey nodded. He stopped, looked carefully at the steps they were climbing, and continued.

Mr. Kingman reached the second floor and started down a walkway. Jeffrey and Pablo followed. Jeffrey walked slowly, his eyes on the floor of the walkway.

"What is it?" Pablo whispered.

Before Jeffrey could answer, Mr. K. stopped in front of a large window and tapped his knuckles against the glass. "This is it. This is my window. The one that was smashed."

Jeffrey stepped forward and examined the window.

"That's all new glass, obviously," said Mr. Kingman. He watched as Jeffrey traced his finger along the window's edge, studying every inch. The boy's serious look brought a smile to the teacher's face. "Okay?" he said.

Jeffrey nodded and stepped back. Mr. Kingman unlocked the front door to his apartment and swung the door open. "Gentlemen, meet the crime scene." The boys stepped past him and filed inside.

Mr. K. stepped in behind them, closed the door, and pointed to a small desk. "That's where I had my laptop. And my stamp collection was next to it, on this table." He stepped across the room and rapped his knuckles on a tabletop next to the desk.

"The police said I should have kept my stamps locked up or hidden away, instead of out in the open, but I never expected a burglary. They said when the thief took my laptop, the sight of my stamp collection was too tempting to pass up."

He shook his head sadly. "Now the loss of my laptop I can live with. It's replaceable. But I've had that stamp collection since I was a boy. It's a family heirloom, and not only that, it's worth money. I'm estimating it's worth around fifty thousand dollars. I'd sure love to get those stamps back."

"Your stamp collection was worth that much?" Pablo asked.

"Oh, yes. Stamps are like a lot of other collectibles. They only go up in value. I had some rarities and errors, and quite a collection, if I do say so myself."

"Do you specialize, Mr. Kingman?" Jeffrey asked.

The teacher swelled with pride. It was a question only a fellow collector would ask. "In United States commemoratives. I didn't know you were a collector, Jeffrey."

"I'm not a collector, but I've read about stamps and stamp collecting. Who knew about your collection?"

"Not a soul."

"Are you sure?"

"I'm positive. I'm what some people call a lone wolf. I don't have many friends, and I really don't socialize all that much."

Jeffrey nodded and pointed to a flat screen television on the wall. "Was that here when the burglary happened?"

"Sure was. I guess I'm lucky that wasn't stolen, too."

Jeffrey noticed some magazines on a table and asked about them.

"I subscribe to those," said Mr. K. "They're stamp magazines, for collectors of American commemoratives. One magazine is from New York, and the other is published in the Midwest."

Jeffrey leafed through the magazines and looked over some of Mr. K.'s mail that was scattered on the table. When he finished, he set everything back in place on the table, sat quietly on the sofa, and stared into space.

Mr. K. leaned close to Pablo's ear and whispered, "What's he doing?"

"Shhh," said Pablo. "Jeffrey's thinking."

Mr. Kingman waited, and waited. He chuckled nervously. Finally, he broke the silence and said, "Well, Sherlock, what do you think?"

Jeffrey blinked and turned to Mr. Kingman. "I think it's a simple case of logic. Whoever broke into your apartment was after your stamp collection. Stealing your laptop was just a diversion to throw the police off."

"But nobody knew about my stamp collection. I already told you that."

Jeffrey picked up the stamp magazines and waved them in the air. "Your mail carrier does. And mailmen have passkeys to lockboxes to get into apartment buildings like this so they can make their deliveries. And while a drug addict or a gang member would look totally out of place in this neighborhood, a mail person wouldn't look suspicious at all. Most people never even notice mail carriers. They could enter the building carrying an empty box, and leave with a full box, and no one would know the difference. They would assume he was delivering or returning a package."

Pablo smiled wide. Mr. Kingman plopped down in a chair across from Jeffrey and stared at the boy. "That's the craziest thing I've ever heard."

"Not really," explained Jeffrey. "A mail carrier could tell from your letters that you're a school teacher who works in the daytime. A smart mailman would also know when all your neighbors would be at work, so he could pick the perfect time to break into your apartment with no fear of getting seen or caught. And like I said, he could walk out of the building carrying a box with your stamps and your laptop inside and no one would notice him."

Mr. K. blinked. "Well, Jeffrey, if you're right, you're a genius. But how do you know if you're right?"

"He's right," said Pablo.

Mr. Kingman looked from Jeffrey to Pablo, and back to Jeffrey again.

"It's the only logical answer," Jeffrey said. "A drug addict or a gang member would have stolen your flat screen long before they took your stamp collection. Someone like that wouldn't even come up here at all. They would have picked an apartment on the first floor, close to the way they came in. None of those facts add up. I'd say the possibility of a drug addict or a gang member committing this crime is close to zero. And, to quote Sherlock Holmes, when you eliminate the impossible, all that remains, no matter how improbable, must be the truth. The thief was someone who knew about your stamp collection and planned to steal it. That leaves only one suspect."

Pablo whistled. "Way to go, Jeffrey!"

Mr. K. hopped to his feet. "What about the blood? There was blood all over my table and desk, and all over the broken glass on the floor. Doesn't that sound like a desperate thief? Like an addict or a gangbanger? That's what the police said."

"I didn't see any blood outside your apartment, or on the walkway or stairs," Jeffrey said. "Was there any blood out there on the day of the crime?"

Pablo snapped his fingers. "That's what you were looking for outside!"

Mr. K. shook his head. "No. No, come to think of it, there wasn't."

"Well," said Jeffrey, "if the thief was bleeding, wouldn't they have dripped blood all the way down your walkway and down the stairs?"

"Logically, yes. But maybe they wrapped their hand in their shirt or something. I don't know."

"If you want to talk logic, Mr. Kingman, the act of stealing itself is illogical. The thief steals more from himself than he does from the person he steals from."

"Why didn't the police think of any of this?"

Jeffrey shrugged.

"And whose blood was that all over my apartment?"

"That's a good question. Based on the evidence, my theory is it didn't belong to the thief. It was probably planted to throw the police off. It might not even be human blood. It might be fake blood. It might be animal blood."

"Animal blood?"

"Did the police test it?"

"They took some samples, but I haven't heard back. To them, this is just a minor crime. To me, it's a nightmare."

"Why don't you ask them what they found?"

Mr. Kingman laughed. "You want me to call the police and ask if they found animal blood in my apartment?"

He turned to Pablo for reassurance, but Pablo shrugged and said, "I would."

Mr. K. laughed again. "Forgive me for saying this, Jeffrey, but this whole mailman/blood theory of yours is a crackpot idea."

"Why?"

"You really think a thief would go to the trouble of planting blood to throw the police off? And a mailman, no less?"

"A clever thief would. Some thieves are clever, despite their stupidity."

Mr. K. chuckled. "Good one. But then our clever thief's not clever enough to plant any blood on the walkway or stairs?"

"Obviously not."

Mr. Kingman scratched his head and sat next to Jeffrey on the sofa. "Gentlemen, I've enjoyed our morning game of playing amateur sleuth, but I think I'll stick with the police investigation. They're the professionals."

Jeffrey's face paled. "But Mr. Kingman, my theory is the only one that makes sense!"

"Are you kidding me? Your theory makes as much sense as a cat wearing pajamas." He held up his hand. "Jeffrey, I have the utmost respect for your intelligence. Every teacher knows you're the smartest kid in school, but this blood business is just too much."

Jeffrey felt a twisting knot in his stomach. His lips quivered and he looked like he was about to throw up.

"Are you okay, Jeffrey?" Pablo said.

From outside the apartment, came a grating, metallic sound. Mr. Kingman sat up sharply. "Did you hear that?"

"What is it?" Pablo asked.

Mr. K. gestured at the window with his hand. "There's a row of mailboxes in the courtyard downstairs."

Pablo nodded. "We saw them when we came in."

"Well, I just heard them open. That means he's here right now: the mailman."

Jeffrey sat up like he'd been hit with an electric jolt. "Then we can prove my theory."

"Prove it how?"

"By questioning him."

"Questioning him? You can't do that, it's too dangerous!"

"Why? You said it was a crackpot idea."

Mr. K. stammered. "Well, maybe I'm wrong. Maybe he is the thief. Look, I'm confused. I don't know what to think right now. What do you say, Pablo?"

"When it comes to mysteries, I trust Jeffrey."

"Maybe you're right, Jeffrey," the teacher conceded. "Maybe the mailman is the thief."

"There's only one way to find out. Come on, Pablo!"

The boys rushed for the door.

"Wait!" cried Mr. Kingman. "I'm coming with you!"

Chapter 3

They found the mailman alone in front of the apartment building's mailboxes, shoveling letters into the appropriate slots. He was a husky black man, with a trimmed beard and a heavy canvas mail bag slung over his shoulder.

The two boys and their teacher crouched behind bushes in the courtyard and watched him. "I feel like we're the criminals now," Mr. K. whispered, "spying on people like this."

"I'll go talk to him," Jeffrey whispered back.

"What?! You can't do that!" He turned to Pablo. "Pablo, help me out here."

"Jeffrey knows what he's doing."

"No, he doesn't."

"Yes, he does."

"He does not."

"He's gone."

Mr. K. spun around. Jeffrey was on his way across the courtyard. "Shoot! This is ridiculous. I feel like an idiot!"

Pablo shushed him and said, "I told you Jeffrey knows what he's doing."

"You better be right," was the grim reply.

Jeffrey stopped twenty feet from the mailboxes and hesitated. Up to this point, he had been occupied with arranging clues in a logical sequence, but now he was about to engage a potential criminal. If the man before him actually was the thief who broke into Mr. Kingman's apartment, then he was both clever and dangerous. Jeffrey knew Pablo and Mr. Kingman were watching. It was on him now. It was all on him.

He stepped forward. "Excuse me," he said, with a high-pitched English accent. "Excuse me, please."

Behind the bushes, Mr. Kingman twitched nervously. "What's he doing? Where'd he learn to talk like that?"

Pablo grabbed his teacher by the arm and turned to him with eyes that said: Don't say a word!

Jeffrey stepped closer. "Excuse me, are you the postman?"

The man gave Jeffrey a glance over his shoulder and continued shoveling letters. He was huge, almost three times as big as Jeffrey, and he spoke with an African accent. "What does it look like?"

Jeffrey had a keen ear for voices and dialects, but the man's accent eluded him. It reminded him vaguely of a substitute teacher he'd had in the seventh grade from Nigeria. "Yes, I suppose you are," he said. "Perhaps you can help me. You see, I'm on holiday and I'm looking for some American stamps for my collection."

The man flinched, but continued feeding letters into the slots. "The post office is down the street."

Jeffrey caught wind of the man's cologne and his nostrils flared. It was a rich, exotic scent. "No, you don't understand. I'm a collector and I fancy American commemoratives from the early 20th century."

The man slammed the row of metal mailboxes shut so hard they shook. He removed his key and spun around to face Jeffrey. "Why you bother me? Can't you see I'm working?"

"I'm sorry to disturb you, but I thought you could help. My father is a magistrate in England and he gave me ten thousand British pounds to buy my stamps. In American currency I believe that's sixteen thousand dollars. At least that's what they told me at the exchange bank this morning. So you see, I'm rather flush right now and I'm really desperate to buy some stamps."

The man's face hardened and his accent thickened. "You are desperate?"

"Quiet desperate. Stamps mean everything to me. Why, I love stamps so much that I'd even consider stealing them."

The man stared at Jeffrey for a moment, his eyes narrowing, then lunged forward with a grunt and seized him by the throat. Jeffrey gasped and grabbed at the man's hands.

Pablo was out from behind the bushes and sprinting across the courtyard. He leapt on the man's back and wrapped an arm around the thick, bearded neck.

Mr. Kingman was a second behind. He threw himself against the man and grabbed at his hands, trying to pry them off Jeffrey's neck, all the while shouting, "Call 9-1-1! Call 9-1-1!"

The four of them struggled, stumbled, and collapsed on the stone walkway. Jeffrey hit the ground first, the man's two hundred-plus pounds on top of him, and Pablo and Mr. Kingman on top of the man. The man's thumbs dug into the hollow at the base of Jeffrey's throat and pressed in hard. Jeffrey jerked and shuddered. His limbs wanted to kick and claw, but he was crushed under the weight on top of him. He heard

Pablo shouting, "Let him go!", and Mr. Kingman shouting, "Call 9-1-1! Call 9-1-1!", and the man's African curses. His vision clouded over and went black. He felt himself going under for the third time. The smell of the man's cologne was overpowering.

Doors opened. Footsteps slapped against pavement. A siren wailed in the distance, drawing closer. Pablo dug the inside of his elbow into the man's windpipe and pulled as hard as he could. The man wheezed. His neck arched back.

Male tenants arrived, grabbing the man by the arms. Together with Pablo and Mr. Kingman, they pulled the man off Jeffrey and pinned him down. Police officers swarmed in and took over. In seconds, the mailman was handcuffed.

Jeffrey sat up on the walkway, coughing and sucking in great gusts of air. Pablo sat next to his friend and patted him on the back. "You okay, Jeffrey?"

Jeffrey nodded and gasped for air. Mr. Kingman sat next to them. His knees were scraped and bleeding, and his hands trembled. Pablo smiled wide and gave his teacher a slap on the back. "Crackpot idea, huh, Mr. Kingman?"

Chapter 4

"Are you insane, Jeffrey? Don't you realize you could have been killed?"

Jeffrey's father sat across from him at the kitchen table. His mother stood facing them, her back against the stove and her arms folded across her chest.

"I'm sorry," Jeffrey said.

"Sorry isn't good enough."

Jeffrey glanced at his mother. She stood stoically, watching him, not speaking. Why wasn't she speaking?

His father leaned back in his chair and threw up his hands in a futile gesture. "How are your mother and I supposed to trust you after a stunt like this? Huh? Answer me that?"

Jeffrey had no answer. He hung his head.

"Answer me, Jeffrey."

"I solved a crime. I thought I was doing the right thing."

His father slammed his fist down on the kitchen table. "The right thing? *The right thing?* You want to know what the right thing is? The right thing is not giving me and your mother a heart attack! That's the right thing!"

Jeffrey stared down at the kitchen table. He'd been yelled at before, but never like this. And why was his mother just standing there and not defending him? Hadn't he helped capture a dangerous criminal? Hadn't the police done a search of the man's apartment and recovered Mr. Kingman's stamps, along with stolen merchandise from dozens of neighborhood burglaries? He touched his neck, still swollen and bruised. Didn't he deserve a medal for what he went through? If I ever have kids, he thought to himself, I'll never yell at them like this. He saw himself surrounded by boys, his own age and younger, gazing up at him in admiration for an act of heroism he'd just performed, asking him questions, wanting to know all the details.... His father's angry voice snapped him back to reality.

"Are you listening to me, Jeffrey?"

"Yes."

"Then look at me when I talk to you! Look me in the eye, like a man!"

Jeffrey met his father's gaze.

"Am I getting through to you? Am I making sense?"

"I guess so."

"Ahh!" His father waved disgustedly and pushed back from the table. His face looked hot and flushed. Jeffrey imagined that if someone had thrown a bucket of water on his father just now, he'd have sizzled.

His father paced the room. "Do you know what it's like to get a phone call from the police department 'regarding your son, Mr. Jones'? Let me tell you something, it scared me half to death. Your mother, too."

Jeffrey glanced at his mother and a surge of guilt racked his body. "But the guy was a thief."

His father spun around and smacked the table again. "I don't care what he is! This is about your safety! Can't you get that through your thick skull? And not just you. Oh, no. What about Pablo? Did you stop to think what might have happened to him? What if he'd been hurt or killed? How would you like that? And that teacher of yours – that Mr. Swingman ..."

"Kingman."

"Him, too. Boy, oh, boy, is he going to hear it from me!"

"Don't yell at Mr. Kingman," Jeffrey pleaded. "He's one of my favorite teachers."

"I'll yell at whoever I want to yell at!"

Jeffrey's mother finally spoke up. "Brad," she said quietly, "why don't you sit down?"

Mr. Jones didn't sit, but he stopped pacing and softened his tone. "Look, Jeffrey, I'm not trying to be a jerk here, but I'm upset because you didn't think about your safety, or the safety of others around you. You didn't use common sense. You of all people. I thought you were smart."

Jeffrey stopped breathing. Of all the things his father had said, that was the most hurtful.

"Jeffrey," said his mother, "your father and I are planning a little trip next month for our anniversary. You know that. We've been discussing it for weeks. How are we supposed to trust you after something like this? How can we leave you here alone even for a short trip?"

"You can trust me."

"Oh, sure," said Mr. Jones. "We can trust you. We'll come home and the whole house will be burned down."

Jeffrey stared down at the table again. Why did his parents always treat him like he was still a little kid? Why did he always feel and act like a kid when he was around them. He didn't feel that way around other people. He turned to his mother. "You can trust me,

Mom. I'll take care of the house. I'll stay home. I won't go anywhere."

"You bet your butt you won't go anywhere," said Mr. Jones. "You're grounded."

"Grounded?" Jeffrey was aghast.

"That's what I said: grounded. For life."

Jeffrey sat with his mouth agape. His father had just dropped the atom bomb.

Jeffrey and Pablo compared notes as they walked to school on Monday morning.

"My dad yelled for two hours," said Pablo.

"My dad yelled for four hours," said Jeffrey.

"My dad was so mad he couldn't see straight."

"My dad was so mad he had steam coming out of his ears."

"My dad grounded me for two days."

"My dad grounded me for life."

Pablo stopped walking and stared at Jeffrey. "For life?"

"That's what he said. He did let me go to church yesterday."

"Yeah, so did my dad."

Beaming like a proud parent, Mr. Kingman leaned back in his chair and repeated the story to his eighth grade math class for the umpteenth time. "... and then Jeffrey says to me, he says, 'But Mr. Kingman, my theory is the only one that makes sense!' "

Laughter filled the room.

Jeffrey squirmed in his seat. He was happy that someone appreciated what he and Pablo had done, but embarrassed by all the attention.

"Jeffrey!" a girl cried. "Do your English accent!"

Jeffrey frowned and shook his head.

Other voices chimed in: "Come on, Jeffrey! Come on!"

Pablo raised his hand. "This is how he talked." Trying his best to imitate Jeffrey's English accent, Pablo said, "I say my good man, are you the postman?"

The class exploded with laughter.

Pablo continued: "It's stamps I want, old boy! Stamps! For my collection!"

Laughter bounced off every wall. Kids pounded their thighs and desktops with their fists. Others clutched their sides, which ached from laughing so hard. Even Jeffrey smiled.

Brian sat fuming. He raised his hand. "Mr. Kingman, do we have to keep going over that story? I thought this was a math class."

Mr. Kingman, still laughing, said, "Well, that's a first, Brian. I never thought you'd be so eager to study math."

"I'm tired of hearing that story over and over."

Pablo turned in his desk to face Brian. "Jeffrey solved a crime. How many crimes have you ever solved?"

"The same as you, Reyes. None."

Pablo's face flushed an angry red.

Brian stood up and pointed at Jeffrey. "Jones, if you're so smart why don't you start your own detective club?" He'd meant it to be funny, but no one laughed.

Pablo stood up. "Why don't you leave him alone?"

"Why don't you make me?"

"Knock it off, both of you!" snapped Mr. K. "Brian, you picked a poor time to pick on Jeffrey. As far as I'm concerned, he's a hero. So is Pablo."

The class exploded with applause and whistles.

Brian slumped back into his desk and sat there stewing.

Pablo smiled from ear to ear.

Jeffrey felt the eyes of the entire class on him. He stared down at the floor, wishing it would open up and swallow him whole.

As the boys walked home from school, Jeffrey said, "Thanks for sticking up for me, but don't get in a fight with Brian McHugh. He's nothing but a simpleton."

"What's a simpleton?" Pablo asked.

"The village idiot."

Pablo laughed.

"Brian is right about one thing, though, Jeffrey."

"What's that?"

"We should start a detective club."

Chapter 5

"Raise your right hand," said Jeffrey, "and repeat after me: I, state your name ..."

"I, state your name."

"No, state your name. *Your* name."

"Oh, I, Pablo Reyes ..."

"Do solemnly swear to uphold the laws and traditions of the North Hollywood Detective Club."

"What laws and traditions?"

"I haven't written them out yet. Just say 'I do.' "

"I do."

"Very well. By the power vested in me, as one of the club's founders, I hereby declare you an official member. Congratulations."

Jeffrey extended his hand to Pablo and they shook. No longer grounded, the boys were in Jeffrey's basement on the first day of summer vacation. The basement served as Jeffrey's bedroom, his private haven from the outside world. The floor was carpeted and the walls were wood paneled. There was no sunlight, a fact which Jeffrey hated, but he had a pair of powerful lamps to use when he wanted to read, which was often. Books spiked out of his bookcase and lay in piles on the floor. There were books on top of chairs and on the seat of a small two-seated sofa, books on Jeffrey's desk, even books on his bed, which was no more than a mattress on the floor.

"All right, now it's your turn," Pablo said.

They reversed roles and Pablo swore Jeffrey in.

"Here, I made these up," Pablo said. He reached in his pocket and pulled out a stack of business cards, held together by a rubber band. He peeled one of the cards out of the stack and handed it to Jeffrey. The card read:

THE NORTH HOLLYWOOD DETECTIVE CLUB
Investigation and Deductive Reasoning
Senior Detective: Jeffrey Jones
Assistant Detective: Pablo Reyes

"Pablo, this is great! But why does it say 'Senior Detective' by my name and 'Assistant Detective' by yours?"

Pablo shrugged and looked at the floor. "You're the smart one. It's not fair for us to be equal when you're the one who always solves everything."

Jeffrey waved his arm as if to dismiss the whole idea. "That's ridiculous. In this club we're both senior detectives."

"No, not really. Brian's right. I've never solved a crime, or a mystery, or even a simple puzzle. I've never solved anything."

"Don't listen to that fool."

"He's right, Jeffrey. You're smart and I'm not."

"You're way smart, Pablo. Way smarter than that idiot McHugh."

"Let me solve a case and then we'll be equal detectives."

"Man, that's crazy. That mailman would have killed me if it wasn't for you. You saved my life. That's why we make a good team."

A woman's scream erupted from the street outside. A scream of pure terror.

Jeffrey and Pablo looked at each other, then dashed for the basement stairs, clomping up the wooden boards.

Outside, the sun beat down with an oppressive heat. The boys stepped out of Jeffrey's air-conditioned house and into a furnace. Their sweat glands opened immediately and their shirts sucked in and clung to their bodies. Blinded by the midday sun, they squinted and blinked as their eyes adjusted.

Half-a-dozen police cruisers lined the street in front of them, red and blue lights popping silently atop their hoods. A swarm of police officers were on foot on the street and sidewalk. The boys heard the scream again. Their eyes swept to the house next door, where a pair of grim-faced officers, one male and one female, escorted a trembling, long-haired boy, hands cuffed behind his back, to one of the waiting police cars. Jeffrey recognized the boy as his neighbor, nineteen-year-old Victor Rodriguez.

Just inside her front door, Victor's mother, a stout woman with ham-like arms, screamed his name and tried to push her way past her thirteen-year-old daughter, Marisol.

"Mom, no!"

The male officer opened the back door to the police car, placed his hand on Victor's head, and guided him into the back seat of the car. The car door closed with a click. From the house came another scream.

Mrs. Rodriguez shoved Marisol out of the way, slapped open the screen door, and tore free from the house in a mad scramble towards the car holding Victor.

"Mom, don't!" cried Marisol.

Officers braced to defend themselves. One reached for his service revolver. The female officer pulled her nightstick and drew back to strike.

"Mrs. Rodriguez!" Jeffrey yelled. He and Pablo dashed for the street and corralled her before she could reach the officers. Each boy grabbed an arm, surprised by her strength and ferocity. Mrs. Rodriguez howled like a wounded animal.

"Better get her out of here," warned the female officer, still brandishing her nightstick.

Marisol ran up behind her mother and locked her arms around the woman's waist. "Help me get her inside!" she said to the boys.

Mrs. Rodriguez wailed and thrashed about. Pablo took a rap on the nose. Jeffrey's glasses were knocked sideways. Marisol pulled with all her strength. Slowly they dragged the hysterical woman across the yard. "They're taking my baby to jail!" she cried.

The front door to the house was open. Marisol reached behind her with one hand for the screen door and yanked it open. She pulled, the boys pushed. Together they got Mrs. Rodriguez through the doorway.

Inside the house with her mother, Marisol slammed the door shut.

The boys stepped back on the porch, drenched in sweat and puffing like steam engines. They heard screaming and shouting from inside the house and another door being slammed. On the street, the police cars were pulling away and turning on their sirens.

Hearing the sirens, a neighborhood dog began to howl. Another dog joined in, and another. In a moment, the whole neighborhood was yelping. The boys frowned and covered their ears.

A bull-necked police officer, sitting in the front seat of one of the squad cars, fixed Pablo with a penetrating stare. Pablo stiffened and stared back. The officer kept his eyes on the boy until the car turned the corner and disappeared. Pablo shivered and turned to Jeffrey, who was studying the last of the police cars as it disappeared down the street, its siren fading out. "What was that all about?"

Before Jeffrey could respond, the door behind them opened and Marisol stepped out, pulling the front door closed and holding the screen door open. She was a pretty girl, but fatigue had weathered her looks. Her angular body slumped against the door frame. Like

Pablo, she had brown eyes and light brown skin. Strands of long black hair covered her face. She swept them back with her hand and lifted her chin and the boys could see that she'd been crying.

"What happened?" Pablo asked her.

"The police arrested my brother, Victor. They said he stole a painting from his boss, but Victor would never do that."

From inside the house came a moanful wail. "Marisol!"

"I'm coming!"

"Marisol, get in the house!"

Marisol ignored the cry. She looked from Pablo to Jeffrey and back to Pablo again. "Can you guys get Victor out of jail?"

"Marisol!" screamed the house.

"I'm coming!" Marisol screamed back. She turned to the boys. "Please, we need your help! You guys found the man who robbed Mr. Kingman. Can you find the person who stole the painting from Victor's boss?"

"Marisol!"

Marisol yanked the front door open and yelled inside. "Wait!" She slammed the door shut and stepped into the front yard. "Come here," she said to the boys. They followed her to the shade of a lemon tree.

"Victor works for a man named Joe Weeden," Marisol explained. "He owns a pawn shop on Lankershim."

"Victor works in the pawn shop?" Pablo asked.

"No, at his house. Cutting grass, watering the lawn, like that. Every Saturday he's there. The police said he stole the painting while he was working, but I know he didn't do it."

"How do you know?" asked Jeffrey.

"He's my brother!" Marisol said, as if that decided it.

"I'm sorry," Jeffrey said. "Go on. Where's the painting now? Did the police find it?"

"No, they tore our house up and didn't find anything. They said Victor hid it somewhere, or sold it already, but Victor doesn't have any money."

"Did the police say anything else? Anything you can remember about Victor or the painting?"

"They said it would be easier for him if he told them where the painting was, but Victor never took it."

Jeffrey nodded. "Has Victor ever been arrested before?"

Marisol lowered her eyes and spoke softly. "He was arrested once in high school. He had some bad friends then, but he's not with them anymore."

"What about a lawyer?"

Marisol sniffled and wiped her eyes. "We don't have money for a lawyer."

Concern for the girl filtered over Pablo's face. He looked to Jeffrey for guidance, but Jeffrey showed no emotion. He merely shrugged and said, "Then he'll get a public defender. Some are good, some aren't."

Horror stared back at them. "Please, you have to help us! Victor didn't do it! He's innocent!" Marisol reached out impulsively and grabbed Pablo by the arm. "Pablo, can you help me?"

The girl's touch startled Pablo. He fumbled his words before managing to say, "We'll do what we can. Right, Jeffrey?"

Jeffrey nodded. The door to the house opened and Mrs. Rodriguez stepped out, her pudgy face stained with tears. "Marisol!"

Marisol and the two boys spun around.

"Get in the house!"

Marisol ran back to the porch, ducked past her mother and slipped inside the house. "Don't talk to anyone!" Her mother told her. "Understand? No one!" Mrs. Rodriguez turned to Jeffrey and Pablo with a belligerent stare. "This is none of your business! Go home!" She stepped back inside the house, slammed the door and locked it.

The boys looked at each other. "Looks like we have our first case," Jeffrey said.

Chapter 6

It was a long, hot bike ride to the pawn shop on Lankershim Boulevard. Jeffrey and Pablo wiped the sweat from their faces and chained their bikes to the iron security bars outside the shop's window. Above them a neon sign said "Weeden Pawn." The shop's old wooden door creaked as they pulled it open and stepped inside.

The pawn shop was small, dusty and cluttered. Televisions, computers, guitars, stereo speakers, boom boxes, and every kind of junk imaginable was piled up high to the ceiling. Most of it looked like it hadn't been touched in years. There was a musty smell about the place, like that of old cardboard.

An older boy in his late teens slouched behind the counter, glaring at the two visitors. He had a shaved head, sinewy muscles, and a plastic patch scotch-taped to the side of his upper arm, covering a fresh tattoo. He looked like trouble.

"Is Mr. Weeden here?" Jeffrey asked with a husky voice, trying to sound older.

"Who are you?" the boy shot back.

Pablo handed him one of their business cards. The boy looked at the card and scowled. "What is this, a joke?"

"We're here to see Mr. Weeden," Jeffrey said firmly.

The boy's face reddened and a pair of veins on each side of his neck seemed to quiver and rise. Just as he looked ready to explode, a raspy, middle-aged voice came from the back of the shop. "I'm Mr. Weeden."

Jeffrey and Pablo turned to see a stoop-shouldered man slouching his way towards them. He had puffy white hair and eyebrows, and wore glasses. He reminded the boys of a picture of Albert Einstein that they had seen in their science textbooks. "What do you want?" he said.

"We're sorry to bother you, Mr. Weeden," Jeffrey said. "We're friends of Marisol Rodriguez, the sister of Victor Rodriguez and - "

Mr. Weeden took a sudden step back. "I don't want any trouble!" he snapped. "I'll call the police if you start any trouble! Eddie!"

The boy reached under the counter, pulled out a leather blackjack, and slapped the lead-filled end of the weapon against the palm of his hand.

Pablo grabbed Jeffrey by the arm with one hand and curled his other hand into a fist, bracing for an attack. Jeffrey spoke quickly, "We're not here to cause trouble, sir. We're investigating a case."

Eddie handed the boys' business card to Mr. Weeden. "That's a temporary card," Jeffrey said. He and Pablo exchanged a look.

Mr. Weeden looked at them both strangely, then he read the card and his bushy white eyebrows rose halfway up his forehead. "Detectives, huh?"

"Yes, sir," Jeffrey said. "If we may, we'd like to ask you a few questions about the painting that was stolen. We promise we won't take long."

Mr. Weeden grunted. "Well, you're interrupting my nap time, but come on." He pulled a set of keys out of his jacket pocket and shuffled to the back of the shop. Jeffrey and Pablo followed him, glancing cautiously over their shoulders to make sure Eddie wasn't behind them.

"I take a nap every day at this time, twelve noon on the dot," Mr. Weeden said. "You'll do the same when you get to be my age."

He unlocked a door and led the boys into a small office. The room was even more cluttered than the shop, with the same cardboard smell. An ancient fan, with fluttering red ribbons tied to its grill, groaned and creaked in the corner. A bare cot with a rumpled quilt took up most of the room's space. As they squeezed inside, Jeffrey bumped against a bicycle.

"Careful," warned Mr. Weeden. "That's Eddie's bike, and you don't want to get on Eddie's bad side."

"No, sir," Jeffrey said, and he didn't.

"We get some characters in here," Mr. Weeden explained. "So I need a tough guy like Eddie up front. He comes in handy sometimes. I don't pay him much, that's why he rides a bike." He chuckled at his stinginess. "Of course, I didn't pay Victor much, either. Maybe that's why the kid stole from me."

The boys watched carefully as Mr. Weeden took off his jacket, draped it over a chair, and lay back on the small cot. He removed his glasses, rubbed the little indentations they made on the side of his nose, and said, "Get on with your questions. I want to take my nap."

Jeffrey took out a pen and an index card from his pocket and began the investigation. "Sir, can you tell us how long you had the painting before it was stolen?"

"About six weeks. Fella who owns the tattoo shop down the street brought it in. Said he was behind on his rent and needed some quick cash. Now that so-and-so was so dumb, he didn't know what he had, but I did. I recognized it immediately: Frances Columbus – 'Flowers of Spain.' That painting's worth half-a-million dollars."

"Half-a-million dollars?" Pablo exclaimed. "For a painting?"

"Oh, yes. And that's a conservative estimate."

"Sir, how much did you give the tattoo shop owner for the painting?" Jeffrey asked.

Mr. Weeden bristled and leaned up on an elbow. "That's none of your business." After a moment, he grumbled and lay back down on the cot. "Let's just say I made an advantageous deal and leave it at that." He chuckled quietly.

"What happened next?"

"I kept the painting in the shop for a bit, but he kept coming back and looking at it, you know, the tattoo guy. That made me nervous so I took it home for safekeeping."

"By yourself?" Jeffrey asked.

"No, Victor was here. He comes in on Mondays for his yard money, so I paid him and then I gave him a ride back to the house in my truck. Me, him, and the painting."

"Is that why you suspect Victor stole the painting?"

"Well, who else? He saw me hang it in my study. He knew it was there, and it disappeared on a Saturday, which is the day he works for me. Nothing else was stolen and there was no sign of a break-in. I'll tell you exactly what happened. Victor has a key to my garage to use my lawnmower and gardening tools. So he goes into the garage, and with no one else around, he picks the lock on the door that leads from the garage into the house. Then he slips inside and takes off with the painting. At least, that's what the witness said."

The boys froze like a pair of statues.

"There's a witness?" Jeffrey said.

"Old man Smithers across the street. He didn't see Victor breaking into my house, but he did see him pedaling his bicycle down the street with the painting tucked under his arm. That did it for me. I called the police right away. Victor's a good kid, but a thief's a thief."

Pablo's mind raced. If a witness saw Victor leaving with the painting, then surely he must be guilty. He thought about Marisol and his heart fell.

"Say, you fellas wouldn't know where Victor hid the painting, would you?" asked Mr. Weeden, with a strange tilt to his voice. He leaned up on one elbow and eyed them both suspiciously. "Maybe Victor told you where the painting is. Maybe you're in on it with him, eh? Suppose I call Eddie in here and we all talk it over."

Pablo felt a jolt run up his spine. He didn't want anything to do with that Eddie. Neither did Jeffrey.

"That won't be necessary, sir," he said. "If we find the painting, we'll notify the police."

"You do that, boys. You do that." Mr. Weeden said, and he lay back on the cot and laughed.

Chapter 7

"Let's get out of here!" Pablo said as he reached for the lock on his bike.

He and Jeffrey were out of the pawn shop and back under the blinding sun.

"Hold on," Jeffrey said. "I want to take a look at the tattoo shop Mr. Weeden mentioned."

"What if he sends that Eddie after us?"

"I doubt he'll do that. I mentioned the police to call his bluff. But just to be safe, let's take our bikes with us."

They unlocked their bicycles and walked them down the blistering sidewalk. Jeffrey made notes of the various businesses they passed: a hardware store, a costume and wig shop, a liquor store, and then they reached the tattoo parlor. As they locked their bikes, an unwelcome voice bellowed at them from down the street: "Jones! Reyes!"

The boys turned to see Brian McHugh pedaling a bicycle in their direction. "Great," said Pablo.

"Don't tell him about the case," Jeffrey whispered.

"Don't worry, I won't."

Brian pulled up alongside of them atop a child's bike that sagged under his weight. He wore a cowboy hat and a silly grin. "What are you doing here, Jones? Getting a tattoo?"

"Where did you get that bike?" Pablo asked.

Brian's face flushed red. "Don't worry about it!"

Jeffrey and Pablo knew immediately that the bike was stolen, and Brian knew that they knew. He shifted uneasily on the bicycle seat. "Seriously, are you getting a tattoo, Jones? Now I've seen everything." He laughed spitefully and pedaled off.

The boys watched as he zigzagged the bike down the sidewalk. "What did I tell you?" Jeffrey said. "The village idiot."

Pablo laughed and patted his friend on the back. Together they entered the tattoo parlor.

The shop was deserted. Jeffrey and Pablo ambled around, eyeing the colorful tattoo designs that covered the walls and countertops. There were birds and animals, girls and gangsters, pirates and dragons, hearts and butterflies, stars and planets, famous dead people, and just about any name imaginable. Jeffrey eyed one that said "Mildred Forever" and chuckled to himself. Mildred was his aunt's name.

"Look at these prices!" Pablo whispered. "Two hundred dollars! Three hundred dollars! Four hundred dollars! Tattoos are expensive."

"Expensive and dangerous," Jeffrey whispered back. "Tattoo ink isn't regulated. Some of those red and yellow pigments can decompose into toxins and leach into the bloodstream. Others are contaminated with bacteria."

"Ew! I didn't know that."

"It's funny when you think about it," Jeffrey mused. "Tattoos were given to slaves in ancient Rome and to criminals in Japan in order to brand them as outcasts. In this country, sailors and bikers and convicts got tattoos to be different and to stand out from society. But now people get tattoos because they want to fit in and be like everybody else. Tattoos have gone from being a symbol of rebellion to a symbol of conformity."

"I never thought of it that way," Pablo said.

"I'll never get a tattoo," Jeffrey declared.

"Me neither!"

They heard a light rapping on the window and turned to the sound. Brian stood outside the shop, his nose pressed up against the glass, making monkey faces at them.

"He'll get a tattoo," Pablo said. "Right here – " He smacked the middle of his forehead.

Jeffrey laughed.

A bearded man, with tattoos up and down his arms, and a red bandana around his head, stepped out of a back room. He saw the boys and his face hardened. "No minors in the shop!"

Brian hopped on his bike and pedaled off. Pablo took a step towards the door. Jeffrey turned to the man with a meek and bewildered expression. "Um, excuse me, sir. I'm writing a paper for school about tattoos and their place in society as an art form. Do you, um, do you consider tattoos an art form?"

The man regarded Jeffrey strangely and his face seemed to soften. "Tattoos are an art form," he said, "a living art form."

"But I mean, um, can you compare tattoos to other forms of art, like painting or sculpture?"

"Of course, you can," the man snapped. "Some people believe tattoos are the oldest art form, older than both painting and sculpture. People were inking each other long before they started inking canvas."

Pablo stood dumbfounded. He knew Jeffrey could play smart or dumb, depending on the situation. But he had never seen him play this character before. He watched as the bearded man pulled up a chair and said, "Tell me more about this paper you're writing."

"Um, like I said, my paper is about tattoos as an art form," Jeffrey said, before bluffing his way through a description of the imaginary paper. Then he let the bearded man talk. The man said he was the owner of the shop, and he began a long discourse on horimono – traditional Japanese tattoos; moko – facial tattoos of the Maori tribesmen; and pe'a – body tattoos of the Samoans. From there it was on to Elizabethan art, Victorian art, and the paintings of Pablo Picasso.

Pablo couldn't understand half of what was being said, but Jeffrey nodded his head and commented often enough to give the impression that he knew what the man was talking about. And he took notes as if it was the most important information he'd ever heard.

It was an hour later when the boys walked out of the tattoo shop and back into the afternoon heat. "What did you observe?" Jeffrey asked.

"He seemed to know an awful lot about art," Pablo said.

"Exactly, which means Mr. Weeden was either wrong in his assessment of the man or he was lying to us.

When the tattoo guy first brought the painting to the pawn shop, he probably knew exactly how much it was worth."

Pablo snapped his fingers. "You're right, Jeffrey. But why would he take a painting worth half-a-million dollars to a pawn shop, especially one with such a cheapskate owner like Mr. Weeden?"

"That's a mystery we'll have to solve," Jeffrey said.

As they unlocked their bikes, a slick red sports car pulled up to the curb. The door opened and an attractive young woman in sunglasses got out. She wore a light sleeveless dress, with tattoos on her bare arms. Her hair was dirty blond and pulled back from her face in a ponytail. She paid the boys no mind, brushing past them on her way to the tattoo shop.

Pablo froze and stared after the young woman as she entered the shop. "Jeffrey, look!" he whispered. "It's Brittany James!"

"Who's that?" Jeffrey asked.

"What do you mean 'who's that'? It's Brittany James, the TV actress." Then he remembered that Jeffrey never watched television. "She's in all my aunt's gossip magazines."

"So she's famous?"

"She's famous for getting in trouble. This must be where she gets her tattoos."

They pressed up against the shop window and cupped their hands against the side of their faces to block out the peripheral sunlight. Brittany James appeared to be in a terrific argument with the bearded man, waving her arms wildly. The boys could hear her voice rising, even screaming, but they couldn't make out the words. The bearded man watched her stoically, nodding his head.

"What do you think that's all about?" Pablo asked in a hushed tone.

"She's obviously upset about something."

"Do you think he gave her the wrong tattoo?"

Jeffrey frowned. "It's got to be something more serious than that. Then again, some people are very serious about their tattoos."

They stepped away from the window and Jeffrey shook his head. "There's something very strange about this whole case, Pablo. An innocent man taken to jail ... Supposedly innocent ... At this point, we don't know. A cheapskate pawn shop owner who hires a thug to work for him.... A tattoo shop owner who takes a painting worth half-a-million dollars to the same cheapskate pawn shop owner.... A stolen painting ... A witness to the crime ... And now this.... One thing's for sure: we're really going to have to put our heads together to solve this one."

"I guess you could say this mystery just keeps getting more mysterious," Pablo said.

"Pablo," observed his friend, "I would call that an excellent deduction."

Chapter 8

It was late in the afternoon, but still stifling hot, when the boys returned home. As they pedaled their bikes into Jeffrey's driveway, they spotted Marisol, sitting on the stoop in front of Jeffrey's door, waiting for them. She was wearing shorts and a tank top, showing brown legs and arms, and fanning herself with a newspaper.

"I'm sorry for the way my mom yelled at you guys," she said as Jeffrey and Pablo climbed off their bikes.

"It's okay," Jeffrey replied. "Your mom's under a lot of stress right now. When people are under stress, they sometimes say things they wish later they hadn't said."

Marisol looked relieved. "I'm glad you're not mad."

"We're not mad," Pablo said. He gave her a smile and Marisol smiled back.

"Come on inside with us, Marisol," Jeffrey said.

The boys stowed their bikes in Jeffrey's garage, then the three of them went inside the house and clamored down the basement steps. Jeffrey cleared the books off some chairs and the two-seated sofa, so Pablo and

Marisol could sit. Then he plopped down on a large beanbag chair and sank into it. He was just about to open his mouth, when the door at the top of the stairs creaked open and his mother's voice called down. "Jeffrey?"

Pablo and Marisol froze. Jeffrey lifted a finger to his lips. His friends nodded.

"Yeah, Mom?" Jeffrey called up.

"Your father's not home yet," said the voice, "So we'll be eating late."

"Okay." Jeffrey gave Pablo and Marisol a thumbs-up.

"Who's down there with you?"

Jeffrey frowned and tapped the side of his head. "Pablo and Marisol."

Marisol waved her arms and whispered, "Don't say anything about Victor! My mom doesn't want anyone to know."

Jeffrey nodded.

"Marisol?" Mrs. Jones sounded confused. Though she lived next door, Marisol had never been in their house before. "Marisol from next door?"

"No, Marisol from the moon."

"Very funny. Hi, Marisol. Everything all right at your house?"

"Hi, Mrs. Jones. Everything's fine." She blushed and covered her face with her hands, ashamed at telling a lie.

"Where's my 'hi'?" called Pablo.

"Hi, Pablo."

"Good evening, Mrs. Jones."

Marisol slapped Pablo playfully on the arm.

"Jeffrey we need to talk later. Your father and I are going out of town next weekend."

"I know, Mom."

"Okay. Bye, Marisol. Bye, Pablo."

"Bye, Mrs. Jones," they called.

"Jeffrey, you really should clean up down there before you invite people over."

They heard the basement door close and Marisol breathed a sigh of relief. The boys told her about Eddie and Mr. Weeden at the pawn shop. "He thinks Victor used his keys to get into the garage, and then picked the lock from the garage into the house," Jeffrey said.

"He's lying," Marisol said. "Victor doesn't know how to pick a lock."

The boys looked at each other and each knew what the other was thinking: If they told Marisol about the witness who saw Victor leaving Mr. Weeden's house with the painting, it would destroy all hope she had in his innocence.

Marisol caught their exchange. "What's that?" she said.

"What's what?" said Pablo.

"That look. What are you not telling me?"

Jeffrey jumped in quickly. "We also went to the tattoo shop and talked to the guy who owns it." He told her about the bearded man with the red bandana, and when the conversation turned to Brittany James, Marisol said, "She's always getting arrested! How come people that are famous like that are always so stupid?"

It was a question they pondered and discussed. Jeffrey said that most people let their emotions instead of their brains tell them how to act. "People behave based on what they feel is right or wrong, or what they wish was right or wrong, instead of what really is right and wrong."

Marisol agreed and added that money and fame made a lot of people go crazy. "It's like when they become famous they think they're better than everyone else," she said. "And then they can't think straight."

"I know what you mean," Jeffrey said. "Fame is like a drug that short-circuits their brain."

"Yes!" said Marisol.

Pablo listened carefully and agreed with them both. He said, "If I ever become rich and famous, I'm going to use my money to help people. I'm not going to act like one of those stupid celebrities."

"Me, too," said Marisol.

"Me, three," said Jeffrey.

As Marisol seemed to relax, Jeffrey carefully reached for a pen and the notes he made while questioning Mr. Weeden. "Let me ask you something, Marisol," he said. "Who was Victor hanging out with?"

"Victor doesn't really have any friends," Marisol said. "Like I told you, he got mixed up with some bad people in high school. He was arrested for shoplifting some jeans and other stuff, and he spent three days in juvenile hall. That seemed to wake him up. Since then, he stays by himself and keeps out of trouble. He just works really hard to take care of my mother."

"Does he have any enemies?'

"Victor? No, everyone likes him. I mean, everyone except his ex-girlfriend."

"Ah!" said Jeffrey, drawing the word out like he'd just discovered a great secret.

"What's with that 'ah'?" said Pablo.

"If Victor is innocent, then I'm wondering if anyone had a reason to frame him," Jeffrey explained. He turned to Marisol. "Who was Victor's girlfriend?"

Marisol shrugged. "Her name was Laura something. I don't remember her last name. Oh, wait! I think it was Nixon, or Nicholas, something like that. White girl, blond hair, lots of makeup. She works at the bowling alley. They broke up two weeks ago."

"Two weeks ago?" Jeffrey said. "So that was before the painting was stolen?"

Marisol nodded.

"How did it end?" Jeffrey asked.

"What do you mean?"

"Victor's relationship with Laura: did it end on good terms or bad terms?"

"Oh. She said she never wanted to see him again."

"I'd call that bad terms," Pablo said.

Marisol looked at Jeffrey with questioning eyes. "Do you really think Victor's ex might have tried to get him in trouble like that?"

Jeffrey sat up in his beanbag chair and spoke in an ominous voice. "Heaven has no rage like love to hatred turned; nor hell a fury like a woman scorned."

Marisol looked at Pablo. Pablo looked at Marisol. Together they burst out laughing.

They laughed because it was funny. They laughed because Marisol had never heard a kid who talked like Jeffrey before. They laughed because after a frightful day of tension and stress, it felt good to cut loose. Jeffrey didn't mind. Pablo was his friend and he was used to Jeffrey's quirks and the funny way he talked. Now maybe Marisol would be his friend, too. He smiled and laughed himself.

The three of them were all laughing when an enormous explosion boomed from outside and seemed to rock the foundation of the entire house. It was followed by a loud pop-pop-popping that cracked like gunfire. Marisol screamed and they all hit the floor and covered their heads.

The blasts continued for a good twenty seconds. Then it ended, as suddenly as it began. They peeked up and looked at each other, the sound still echoing in their ears. "Jeffrey!" Mrs. Jones shrieked from upstairs. "Are you okay?"

"Yeah, Mom!"

Outside, a car door slammed and tires screeched. Jeffrey and his friends sprang to their feet and rushed up the basement stairs.

Jeffrey's front yard was dense with smoke and the smell of gunpowder when the trio spilled out of his house. The smoke stung their throats and burned their eyes, causing tears to spill. A sea of shredded paper casings, wrappers, strings, and half-burnt firecrackers lay scattered across the lawn. In the distance, a car's engine faded as it raced away.

Marisol gagged and bent over at the waist to vomit. Pablo patted her on the back and led her away from the smoke. "What was that all about?" he called over his shoulder at Jeffrey.

Jeffrey coughed and wiped his eyes. "I think it's a warning."

"What warning?"

"Someone doesn't want us on this case."

Jeffrey's mother stepped out the front door and fanned the air in front of her face. "What happened?"

Pablo coughed and pulled his shirt up over his nose. "Looks like firecrackers, Mrs. Jones."

"Oh, Jeffrey, not again!"

"What do you mean 'again'?"

"If this is one of your friends," his mother warned.

"It's not my friends."

"Well, then who is it?"

"I don't know."

"Oh, I can't breathe!" She turned back to the house. "Your father is going to hear about this." She stepped inside and closed the door.

"It's not my fault!" Jeffrey called after her, his voice rising.

The front door opened and Mrs. Jones popped her head out. "And clean up this mess!" She pulled her head back inside and slammed the door.

Jeffrey threw up his hands. Marisol remained doubled over, coughing and trying to breathe. Pablo leaned close to her. "Are you okay?" Marisol wiped her eyes and nodded.

Jeffrey trudged to the garage, took a rake, a broom, and a dustpan, and set to work. Pablo took the rake, Marisol took the dustpan, and together with Jeffrey they swept the shreds and remnants of hundreds of firecrackers into a large pile.

"Wow, that's like enough for an army," Pablo said. "Probably some M-80's in there, too. You still think someone was trying to scare us?"

"We don't have any proof," Jeffrey said, "but I don't know why else someone would do this. My great-grandpa was in the Korean War, and he used to say, 'You know you're getting close to the target when you start getting hit by flak.' I'd call this flak."

"What's flak?" Marisol asked.

"Antiaircraft fire."

"I get it."

"It means we're getting close to the truth," Pablo said.

Jeffrey nodded. "Only at this point, we don't know what the truth is."

"Who do you think did it?" Marisol asked.

"We talked to three different people," Jeffrey told her, "Eddie, Mr. Weeden, and the pawn shop guy. But only Eddie and Mr. Weeden saw our business card and know our real names. Take your pick."

"I pick Eddie," Pablo said.

"I agree. But the obvious choice isn't always the right choice. We have no evidence."

The sun was sinking fast on the horizon, casting long shadows across the yard. Mrs. Rodriguez stepped out on her porch and called for Marisol to come home. "I'm coming," Marisol called back. Mrs. Rodriguez saw

Jeffrey and Pablo, and ducked back inside her house, slamming the door.

Marisol handed the dustpan to Pablo. "Please don't tell anyone about Victor."

"We won't tell anyone," Pablo assured her.

"You promise?"

"Sure."

"Jeffrey, you promise?"

"I promise. Don't tell your mom about the firecrackers or anything we talked about."

"I won't," Marisol said, and ran back home.

The boys looked at each other. "Looks like this case is getting serious," Pablo said.

"Yup," Jeffrey said, "serious and dangerous."

Chapter 9

"Firecrackers are not toys," said Jeffrey's father at the dinner table that night. "I don't find this funny at all."

"I'm not laughing," Jeffrey said.

"No, but your friends are."

"It wasn't my friends, Dad. I keep telling you that."

"Then it's your enemies, and that's even worse."

Jeffrey stared at his plate. His parents had him on the defensive again, and he felt like a child in front of them. "I don't know who did it," he mumbled. "Probably just some neighborhood kids, goofing off. If it's that big a deal, I guess I could investigate it."

Mr. Jones slammed his fork down. "And that's another thing. This investigation business and this detective hobby of yours, it has to stop."

Jeffrey shot straight up in his chair. "Why?"

"I don't want you or somebody else getting hurt."

"Nobody's getting hurt!"

"Jeffrey," his mother said, "your father and I are going out of town next weekend. We've had this trip planned for a long time."

"I know, Mom. I know."

"Well, then you must be aware of how concerned we are about leaving you here on your own."

Mr. Jones shrugged. "Maybe we should call the whole thing off."

"Why?" Jeffrey was both shocked and offended that his parents didn't trust him. Hadn't he proven to them, many times over, how responsible he was? "I'll be fine. I can take care of the house."

His parents looked at each other.

"I can. I know what to do. I have the list about feeding the fish, and taking the trash out. I know how to do everything."

"Well ..." his mother said, gazing down at her plate.

Mr. Jones turned to Jeffrey with a serious look. "How do we know those firecrackers aren't from that mailman burglar you helped to catch?"

"He's in jail."

"We hope he's in jail, but we don't know that for sure. These liberal politicians we have running California love nothing better than letting criminals go free. What if it's his friends, out to make trouble for you?"

"Oh, Dad...."

"Don't 'oh, Dad' me. Did you investigate that one?"

"No, but I could."

Mrs. Jones stifled a laugh.

"Look, son," said his father, "there's no doubt in my mind that someday you're going to make a fine police detective. Maybe even commissioner. Maybe even district attorney. But, please, can we at least get you through high school first?"

Jeffrey looked at his food and nodded.

Mr. Jones looked relieved. "Good. Now about a summer job: My friend, Mike Kozlowski, needs some help cleaning garages and mowing lawns. He's paying twenty bucks a garage and twenty bucks a lawn. You interested?"

"Yeah, sure," Jeffrey said, perking up.

"You'll be working with your body instead of your brain, but sometimes that's a good thing."

"How many workers does he need?" Jeffrey asked.

"He said two or three boys. Why, you want to tell Pablo?"

"If it's okay."

"Pablo's a responsible boy," offered his mother.

"You go see Mr. Kozlowski tomorrow morning," said his father. "Wait and see if he hires you first, then tell him about Pablo."

"I will. Thanks, Dad."

As Jeffrey's parents got ready for bed that night, his mother wondered, "Do you really think it's a good idea for Jeffrey to have a job?"

"Sure, why not?" said his father. "He's fourteen-years-old, it's time he learned the value of a dollar. I was working when I was his age. Younger than him, actually. Besides, a job will keep his mind off all this detective nonsense."

"I know, but Mike Kozlowski? Isn't he going to be a little hard to work for?"

"Old Iron Mike? Ah, he's a big softie."

"That's what you think. That man hasn't smiled since Ronald Reagan was in office."

Mr. Jones laughed. "You're probably right, but a boss like that will be good for Jeffrey. It'll toughen him up. I'm too easy on him."

"Oh, really?"

"You don't think so? That kid gets away with murder in this house. And I'm too busy to do anything about it."

"Oh, so it's my fault now?"

"No, it's not your fault. We're both busy."

"I just don't like that Mike Kozlowski," Mrs. Jones insisted. "I've known him since we were married and I've never seen him without a scowl on his face or a mean word on his lips. He never smiles, he never laughs. And the way he talks to people – ordering them around – it's disgraceful. He's nothing but a mean, angry, bitter old man."

"Relax, honey. The boss at your first job is supposed to be a tyrant. At least, mine was. Anyway, it's just a summer job and Jeffrey hasn't even got it yet. He still has to sell himself to the old man."

"Poor Jeffrey," said his mother.

In his room in the basement, Jeffrey kneeled by his bedside and said his nightly prayers. When he finished, he crawled into bed and stared up at the ceiling.

The events of the day played before his mind: Victor getting arrested, the visit to the pawn shop, his conversation with the owner of the tattoo shop, and then the firecrackers....

He thought about what his parents had said at dinner that night. So they thought his friends were the ones who set off the firecrackers? Jeffrey laughed sadly at that one. Except for Pablo, he didn't have any friends. Other kids thought he was strange, and he was. Some of them, like Brian McHugh, were always making fun of him. Would it be that way in high school, too?

He wondered why he was so different and why he couldn't be normal like everyone else, happy just to watch television and play video games. Yet those things bored him to death. He had no idea why mysteries, puzzles, and solving crimes excited him so much, he only knew that they did.

He didn't know why he enjoyed reading so much, either. That was another thing kids made fun of him about. They thought he was weird, because of all the reading he did, but next to solving puzzles and mysteries, there was nothing he liked better than curling up with a good book.

He knew from reading that throughout history many cultures had considered kids his age to be adults. Fourteen-year-olds had fought in wars, got married, and ruled kingdoms. Yet to his parents, he was just an irresponsible kid.

His mind drifted and he thought again about their dinner conversation. He knew his parents were worried about his safety and wanted the best for him, even if they didn't always trust him. He hadn't told them about Victor's arrest, because Marisol had asked them not to tell anyone. If his parents knew, they might make him drop the case. Still, Victor was in jail and maybe Jeffrey could help him. Even if he was a misfit, he knew he was good at solving mysteries and crimes.

He thought and he thought. Was there a way to make everyone happy? What if he continued his investigation, but was extra careful not to put himself in any danger? Then he could satisfy his parents and help Victor at the same time. Maybe that was it. Just when he thought he had found the perfect solution, the telephone in the basement rang.

Jeffrey leaned out of bed and picked it up. "Hello?"

There was no sound, only a faint breathing.

"Hello?" Jeffrey said again.

A girl's voice spoke to him, a voice he did not recognize. "If you're smart," she said, "you'll mind your own business."

Then the line clicked dead

Chapter 10

Mr. Kozlowski sat in his office behind a huge Oak desk and glowered down at Jeffrey. His face was lined and creased from every angle, and when he frowned, which was often, the lines and furrows only deepened.

It made Jeffrey nervous just to look at him. And it didn't help that the tiny chair Jeffrey was sitting in was barely a foot off the floor, making him feel like a midget before the towering older man. His palms were sweaty and he kept wiping them on his pants legs.

Mr. Kozlowski noticed. He lowered his head and glared down at Jeffrey over the top of his glasses. "What's wrong with your hands?"

"Nothing, sir."

"Then keep still."

"Yes, sir."

The older man lectured Jeffrey on his apartment buildings and the garages and properties that he owned. "I'm looking for responsible boys who aren't afraid of hard work. I fired the last one for sleeping on the job, and the one before him for coming in late, and two others before that for pure laziness. I don't stand for laziness, cursing, swearing, or boys who don't want to work. Now give me one good reason why I should hire you."

Jeffrey stammered. "I'm a hard worker, and I learn fast, and I'll do my best at whatever you want me to do."

"That's three reasons. I said give me one."

"Oh. I'm honest."

Mr. Kozlowski studied Jeffrey for a long moment. "Honesty is important," he finally said. He shuffled some papers on his desk. "Your dad tells me you're a good mystery solver."

"Yes, that's true."

"Hmmm. Well, not much use for that in this job. Can you handle a lawnmower?"

"Yes, sir. I cut the grass at my house. I'm good at cutting grass."

Mr. Kozlowski grunted. "How about hard physical work? Cleaning and moving furniture, and so forth. Can you manage that?"

"I guess so."

Mr. Kozlowski sat up straight in his chair and scowled down at Jeffrey. "You guess so?"

"I mean, yes, sir. Absolutely. I can do that."

Mr. Kozlowski removed his glasses and shook his head sadly. "I've been disappointed so many times. I hope you don't disappoint me."

"I won't disappoint you, Mr. Kozlowski. Do I have the job?"

Mr. Kozlowski grumbled and put his glasses back on. "Come back at noon and we'll get started."

"Thank you, sir. How many workers do you need?"

The older man's eyes narrowed suspiciously. "Why do you ask?"

"I have a friend who works real hard."

"I don't hire friends." Mr. Kozlowski turned his attention to the papers on his desk. "Friends lead to horseplay, and horseplay on the job costs me money."

"I can personally vouch for his character," Jeffrey said.

The older man looked up and his eyebrows arched. "Is that so?"

"Yes, sir. He's a good person, and he's honest, and he's strong. He can do a lot of work, more than me probably."

Mr. Kozlowski leaned over his desk and pointed a bony finger down at Jeffrey. "In that case, you tell your friend to be here in one hour sharp. But if he's even half a minute late ..."

Pablo was there in forty-five minutes, pronto, wearing a clean shirt and tie. Mr. Kozlowski grilled him the same as he had Jeffrey. Pablo answered him honestly, and to his surprise, Mr. Kozlowski hired him.

An hour later, the boys found themselves in a dark, dusty garage, filled with rusty tools, old broken-down lawnmowers, shovels, pool cleaning equipment, a grimy work bench, and a refrigerator with a sign taped across its front that said FREE.

"What a mess!" Pablo exclaimed, after Mr. Kozlowski had left. "It looks like Mr. Weeden's pawn shop. No, worse."

"That's what I was thinking," Jeffrey said. "Well, I guess we should start with that old refrigerator." Mr. Kozlowski had told them to roll it out to the sidewalk and leave it there the rest of the day. "No one will take it," he had said. "So at the end of the day, you'll have to bring it back in."

"How do you know no one will take it?" Pablo had asked.

"Because I've been putting it out there every day for weeks, trying to give it away and nobody wants it. I suppose I'll have to pay someone to haul it off."

The boys worked quickly. They started with the refrigerator and then moved everything else outside to the yard. With the garage cleared out, they cleaned the work bench and swept the floor. After a short break, they washed the floor and put everything neatly back in place. Four hours later, they were exhausted and sore, but proud of the job they'd done. It was the hardest either one of them had ever worked.

Mr. Kozlowski returned at the end of the afternoon with a scowl on his face, but one look at the garage and he froze in his tracks. He stared in shock at the clean, shiny floor, the polished work bench, and the tools all arranged in neat and orderly rows. "Why, this is the cleanest garage I've ever seen!" he gushed.

"Yes," Jeffrey remarked, "we took a rough stone and turned it into a polished gem."

Mr. Kozlowski turned to Jeffrey with a look of pure bafflement. "What the doozy did you just say?"

Pablo laughed and Mr. Kozlowski spun angrily on his heels. "What's so funny?"

"Mr. Kozlowski," Pablo managed between laughs, "that's the way Jeffrey talks!"

Mr. Kozlowski turned back to Jeffrey, who held up his hands and shrugged sheepishly. The older man looked from one boy to the other and back again. Slowly, very slowly, a smile creased his worn and tired face. He chuckled quietly, then he laughed, then he roared with delight and pounded the work bench. "A polished gem! Oh, that's a good one!"

The boys joined him and laughter filled the garage. Abruptly, the older man stopped and his eyes darted about the garage. "Wait a minute," he said, "where's the refrigerator? I didn't see it outside and it's not here."

"Somebody took it," Pablo told him. "We don't know who."

"But how? I've been trying to give that thing away for weeks and nobody wants it."

"That was easy," Jeffrey explained. "We figured nobody wanted it, because they thought it wasn't worth anything. So we took that FREE sign off and put the refrigerator out on the sidewalk with a new sign that said FOR SALE $100. It was gone in less than an hour."

The laughter started all over again, even louder this time. "You guys are too smart for me!" the older man howled. "Just too smart!"

Chapter 11

Outside, the sun was blistering. Laughter and praise from Mr. Kozlowski had made the boys forget how hard they'd worked, but as they pedaled their bicycles home, fatigue caught up with them. They slumped over their handlebars, barely hanging on, and every hill brought forth a chorus of groans.

"My legs are sore," Jeffrey moaned.

"My back is sore," Pablo moaned louder.

"My hair is sore," Jeffrey moaned the loudest.

"How can your hair be sore?"

"I don't know, it just is."

Jeffrey told Pablo about the mysterious phone call he received and the words of warning.

"Do you think it was Victor's girlfriend?" Pablo asked. "The one that Marisol told us about."

"That was my first thought," Jeffrey said. "We'll have to question her."

As they finally rolled onto Jeffrey's street, Mrs. Rodriguez drove past them in her car, headed in the opposite direction. She yelled out the car window. "See

Marisol. She has something for you!" Then the car sped off.

The boys glided their bikes into Jeffrey's driveway. Marisol was waiting and waving at them from her front porch. "Hey! Over here!" They stowed their bikes in Jeffrey's garage and trudged over to see her.

"How was work?" she asked.

Jeffrey looked at her, surprised. "How did you know we had jobs?"

Marisol grinned. "I'm a detective, too."

The boys looked at each other, stumped.

"No, actually I came by your house, Jeffrey, and your mom told me." She opened her front door. "Come inside. My mom made some food for you guys."

"She did?" Pablo asked as they followed her through the door. The air conditioned house cooled their bodies and though they had never been in Marisol's home before, it had a comfortable, lived-in feel that put them immediately at ease.

"My mom still feels bad about yelling at you guys," Marisol said, leading them through the living room.

"Tell her not to worry," Jeffrey said. "I'm used to getting yelled at."

Pablo and Marisol laughed. "I told her you were helping us," Marisol said. They reached the kitchen. On the table were two steaming plates of broiled salmon, steamed broccoli, and salad. Jeffrey's eyes lit up. "Is that for us?"

"Yup. Sit down. Eat. I'll be right back." She hurried out of the room.

"Tell your mom thanks!" Pablo called after her.

"Double thanks!" Jeffrey called, even louder.

The boys sat down and dug in. "This is great!" Pablo exclaimed. Jeffrey didn't respond. He was too busy chewing and savoring every bite. "Mm," he finally managed. "It's greater than great."

A minute earlier, their feet had been tired, their legs and backs aching, but now the meal that Mrs. Rodriguez had so lovingly prepared for them was healing their bodies and their spirits faster than any iodine or medicine possibly could.

Marisol entered with a huge stack of magazines and plopped them down on the table. "These are my mom's, but she said you guys could have them. They all have pictures or articles about Brittany James."

The boys looked at each other and then at her.

"I don't know if they'll help at all," Marisol said with a wave of her hand.

"No, that's good thinking, Marisol," Jeffrey told her. "We have to investigate every lead. Now you're thinking like a detective."

Marisol smiled from ear to ear.

Pablo pulled some magazines off the top of the pile and spread them open. Mrs. Rodriguez had tagged the pages featuring Brittany James so they were easy to find. Marisol sat next to him and leaned over his shoulder as he leafed through the pages.

One picture showed Brittany James with a gigantic purse slung over her shoulder as she strode down a sidewalk in Beverly Hills. Marisol stamped the picture with her finger. "Look, that's a three thousand dollar bag."

Pablo was stunned. "Three thousand dollars? For a bag?"

"Yup."

"Look at how big it is," Pablo said. "You could hide like three small children in there."

Marisol laughed. Pablo flipped through more of the pictures, and she leaned in closer. "Do you think Brittany James is pretty?" she asked.

Pablo shrugged. "She's okay."

"Huh!" Marisol said in a superior way.

"What's that 'huh' for?" Pablo asked.

Marisol didn't respond. Instead she pushed off from the table and stalked out of the room.

Pablo turned to Jeffrey with a bewildered look. "What did I say?"

"Don't worry about it. Just eat." Jeffrey had never tasted anything so good. He could eat like this every day for the rest of his life, he decided. "Marisol!" he called, between bites.

"What?" came Marisol's voice.

"Do you have Laura's address?"

The boys heard footsteps and Marisol appeared, leaning against the door frame. "You mean Victor's ex?"

"Yeah. Pablo and I are going to question her tomorrow morning, before we go to work."

Marisol took her seat back at the table, eyes wide. "What are you going to say to her?"

"I haven't decided yet. We'll snoop around, see if she knows anything about Victor and the painting."

"Wait, I'll see if I can find her address in Victor's room!" She bounded out of the kitchen.

"And get Mr. Weeden's home address!" Jeffrey called. "Where Victor worked!"

Pablo looked at Jeffrey and whispered, "Why do you need Mr. Weeden's home address?"

"The witness," Jeffrey whispered back. He lifted a finger to his lips and Pablo nodded.

Marisol called, "I got Mr. Weeden's address, but I can't find Laura's. How about the address to the bowling alley where she works?"

"That's good."

Marisol returned to the kitchen and handed the boys a slip of paper. "That's the address to the bowling alley. Can I come with you guys when you talk to Laura?" she pleaded. "Please?"

Pablo turned to his friend, but Jeffrey didn't miss a beat. "How did you and Laura get along when she was dating Victor?"

"Not so hot."

"Probably better if you didn't come then," Jeffrey said. "We want to catch her off-guard. If she sees you, she might get defensive."

Marisol stuck out her lower lip in a pout, but she nodded and said, "I guess you're right." She handed

Jeffrey another slip of paper. "Here's Mr. Weeden's address. Did you guys tell anyone about Victor?"

The boys shook their heads. "Did you tell anyone about the firecrackers?" Pablo asked.

"No, but my mom asked about them," Marisol said. "She heard all the explosions."

"What did you tell her?" asked Pablo, as Jeffrey took a sip of water.

"I told her Jeffrey had a fiesta."

Jeffrey choked and spit out his water in a spray across the table.

Pablo and Marisol roared with laughter and beat the table with their fists.

At dinner that night, Mr. Jones gave his wife a wink and a knowing smile, and said to Jeffrey, "How was your first day at work, son?"

"It was okay. Mr. Kozlowski sure likes to laugh."

Mrs. Jones dropped her fork with a clang. "That man hasn't laughed in forty years!"

Jeffrey gave his mother a strange look. "Mr. Kozlowski? He laughs all the time."

"Are we talking about the same person?" his mother asked, incredulously.

"I don't know who you're talking about, but I'm talking about Mr. Kozlowski." Jeffrey popped a forkful of salad in his mouth. Mrs. Jones rolled her head and looked at her husband. "I mean, he seems grumpy," Jeffrey added, "but once you get to know him, he's really a nice guy."

"And you know him?" his mother said. "After one day?"

"Yeah, Mom. He's cool. He said me and Pablo can go swimming in one of his pools."

His parents looked at each other. "Now I've heard everything," said his mother.

"I think you have Mr. Kozlowski confused with someone else," Jeffrey said.

Mr. Jones laughed loudly. Mrs. Jones was speechless.

Jeffrey set his fork down. "Dad, can I be excused? Mrs. Rodriguez made some food for me and Pablo, and I'm not very hungry."

"Oh, really?" his mother asked, her eyebrows arched high. "You know, Marisol Rodriguez came knocking on the door this afternoon. Are you two friends now?"

Jeffrey stared at his plate. He wasn't comfortable with his mother asking him about girls. He could feel his face flushing, and was glad when his father said, "Go ahead, son."

Jeffrey pushed off from the table and hurried to his room in the basement.

Mrs. Jones turned to her husband. "I just don't know what to make of that boy. I just don't."

Mr. Jones shrugged. "Maybe old Mike has a heart after all."

"That'll be the day."

Chapter 12

It was early in the morning when Jeffrey and Pablo arrived at the bowling alley where Laura worked, but the lanes hummed and crackled with life. A children's summer league was competing and the air was filled with shouts, squeals, and the clatter of bowling pins being knocked and rattled in their cages.

The boys walked past the refreshment area where popcorn machines pinged and ponged. They inhaled the smell: stale popcorn slathered in imitation butter. Together with the fresh wax on the floor of the bowling lanes, it made for an odd, but unmistakable scent. They spotted a shoe rental counter and approached it.

Behind the counter sat a gum-chewing teenage girl in a red work shirt. She had a phone in her hands, her eyes glued to the screen.

"Excuse me," Jeffrey said. "Is Laura here?"

"Laura's on a break," the girl replied, without looking up.

"Do you know where I can find her?"

"Nope." Her finger glided across the screen.

"Do you know how long her break is?"

"Nope." Another swoosh of her finger.

"When she does come back from her break, do you know where she'll be working?"

"Nope."

"Thanks," Jeffrey said, "you've been a big help."

The girl blew out a big bubble of gum and popped it. "Anytime."

The boys turned away from the counter. "Don't you know sarcasm when you hear it?" Pablo said over his shoulder, but the girl didn't hear him.

"She'll go far in life," Jeffrey said.

"Yeah, right."

They made their way through the bowling alley, stepping carefully as children squealed and scampered around them. Pablo spotted an attractive blond-haired girl, wearing a denim jacket over a red work shirt. She was a few years older than they were, with red nails and lots of makeup, and she was walking directly towards them. Pablo nudged Jeffrey with his elbow and nodded in the girl's direction.

Jeffrey saw her and as the girl approached, he said, "Excuse me, are you Laura?"

"I'm on a break," she snapped, stepping past them.

"Can we talk to you for a second?" Jeffrey called after her.

"I'm on a break!" she repeated, louder this time.

"It's about Victor," Jeffrey said.

Laura stopped in her tracks and turned to face them. "Who are you?"

"We're friends of Victor's sister, Marisol. Victor is in jail."

Laura stepped closer. "What do you mean he's in jail?"

"The police arrested him. We think he's innocent and we want to help him. If you have a minute, we'd like to talk to you."

Laura looked them both over and gave a little wave of her arm. "Come here."

She led them past the refreshment area and through a door marked EMPLOYEES ONLY. An older boy in a red work shirt stepped past them, going in the opposite direction. He saw Jeffrey and Pablo and shouted, "Hey! You can't come back here!"

"It's okay," Laura told him. "They're with me."

The boys followed her into a dimly lit employee lounge area. The space had an old sofa with the stuffing coming out, a couple of fold-out metal chairs, and a candy machine. Laura closed the door and faced them. They were the only ones in the room.

"Tell me what happened," she said.

Jeffrey told her about Mr. Weeden, the painting and Victor's arrest. As she listened, Laura nodded and chewed on her lower lip.

"So that's why we're here," Jeffrey said. "We were hoping you could tell us about your relationship with Victor."

Laura blew out a long breath of air. She reached in the pocket of her denim jacket, pulled out a pack of spearmint gum, and offered a piece to Pablo. He shook his head. "Jeffrey?" she said, offering him some gum.

"No thanks."

Laura unwrapped a piece of gum and popped it in her mouth. "Well, I'm not surprised," she finally said. "I knew Victor was headed for trouble. That's why I broke up with him."

Jeffrey eyed her carefully. "How did you know he was headed for trouble?"

"The way he acted and the people he hung around with. Like if we went to the movies, he'd want to sneak in. Or this one time, we were in a restaurant and after we ate, Victor's like, 'Let's dine and dash.' And I'm like

'No way!' I ended up paying for the dinner myself, because Victor refused to do it. He said I was a fool for paying when we could just walk out without anyone knowing."

"You mentioned his friends," Jeffrey prodded her.

"Yeah. Victor was hanging out with bangers. Gang bangers, you know. They talked a lot about stealing and getting in fights. I didn't like that. So I broke up with him. Like I said, I knew he was headed for trouble and I was right."

"We don't know if he's guilty or not," Jeffrey said.

Laura laughed. "Trust me. He's guilty." She glanced at a clock on the wall. "I gotta get back to work." She opened the door, stopped, and turned around. "Don't waste your time trying to prove Victor is innocent. He's not an angel."

"Wow, that's a whole different side to Victor," Pablo said quietly as they stepped out of the bowling alley. "It sounds like he might really be guilty." He was already wondering how he was going to break the bad news to Marisol.

Jeffrey glanced over his shoulder. There were a couple of people behind them, so he waited until they had walked far enough away so that no one could hear them talk. Then he motioned for Pablo to lean in close and he spoke in a whisper. "There's only one problem with her story. Did you see when she offered me some gum?"

Pablo nodded.

"She called me by name," Jeffrey said.

"So?"

"So we never told her our names or gave her a business card. And I've never met her before in my life. The only way she could have known my name was if someone told her we might be coming."

"You're right!" Pablo exclaimed, a little too loud. Jeffrey shushed him and Pablo lowered his voice. "But who would have told her about us?"

Jeffrey looked at his friend. "It's an easy deduction. Either Eddie, Mr. Weeden, or the tattoo shop owner. And we might have to eliminate the tattoo guy, because we never told him our names or gave him a business card. That leaves only Eddie and Mr. Weeden, our two primary suspects from last night's firecrackers."

Pablo whistled through his teeth. "That's good detective work, Jeffrey. What about Laura's voice? Does she sound like the girl who called you with the warning?"

Jeffrey shrugged. "I couldn't tell. Maybe it was her, maybe it wasn't. Right now, the only thing I know for sure is that everything Laura just told us is probably a lie."

Chapter 13

"I have some lawns that need mowing," said Mr. Kozlowski, "but it's a little too hot for that today, and you guys did such a good job with that last garage, I figured we'd start here."

He opened a heavy garage door, and Jeffrey and Pablo followed him inside. This garage was even messier than the first. It was filled with speakers, sound equipment and musical instruments, all covered in dust and cobwebs.

"Watch out for the spiders," Mr. Kozlowski warned, only half joking. He was dressed in a pair of worn denim overalls and a plaid work shirt. To the boys, he looked like an old country farmer. "I don't know what to do with all these old instruments," he said, as they began sorting through the mess. "I've been trying to sell them on the internet, but no one's buying."

"There's a pawn shop on Lankershim," Pablo said. "The owner's name is Joe Weeden. He might be interested in it."

Mr. Kozlowski laughed. "Joe Weeden! Where do you think I got all this junk?"

"You got it from Mr. Weeden?" Jeffrey asked.

"Sure did. Before he moved to the valley, Joe Weeden had a pawn shop in downtown Los Angeles, but it burned down. That's when I bought all these instruments and this sound equipment. It was a fire sale, literally. But the joke was on me, because I was never able to resell any of it."

"When was this?" Jeffrey asked.

"Close to twenty years ago."

"Maybe you can pawn it back to him now," Pablo suggested.

The older man frowned. "I don't do business with Joe Weeden anymore."

"How come?" Pablo asked.

"Because I don't trust the man. When his shop burned down, he was the number one suspect. Rumor is he torched the place himself."

"Why would he do that?" Pablo wondered.

"Insurance," said Jeffrey.

"That's right, son," confirmed Mr. Kozlowski. "The fire investigators determined it was arson. They just couldn't pin it on Weeden himself. I believe he set fire to his own building. And it wouldn't be the first time. Twice buildings he owned have burned to the ground, and each time he's collected a big settlement."

Jeffrey and Pablo glanced at each other.

"I saw that look," said Mr. Kozlowski. "You boys know something I don't?"

"We're investigating a crime," Jeffrey said, "and Mr. Weeden's name has come up."

"Is that so? Well, when it comes to solving crime, I have one piece of advice: follow the money. You do that, and it'll always lead you to the guilty party."

"What do you mean, Mr. Kozlowski?" Pablo asked.

"It's like this, son: When a crime occurs, the person who benefits, the one who stands to gain the most from the crime, is usually the one who did it. Take the husband who's murdered. If the wife cashes out with a big insurance settlement, more often than not, she had a hand in the killing. That's why I don't trust Joe Weeden. The papers said he doubled the insurance policy on his shop six months before it burned down. Afterwards, he ended up with a pretty hefty payment. Who else had a reason to set his business on fire? No one. Follow the money, boys."

They were interrupted by a shout from the sidewalk outside. "Jones! Hey, Jones! Let me see your tattoo!" It was Brian, sitting atop his tiny bicycle, just outside the garage door.

Mr. Kozlowski peered out at the street. "Who's that loudmouth?"

"His name's Brian McHugh," Jeffrey said.

"He's a bully," Pablo added. "He likes to pick on Jeffrey."

"Is that so?" said Mr. Kozlowski. "I don't like bullies. I was bullied myself when I was a boy. Let me go have a talk with that fellow."

Mr. Kozlowski headed out to the sidewalk. The sun was blistering and bright, and he blinked his eyes as they adjusted. Brian called past him, taunting the boys in the garage. "Jones, take off your shirt so we can see your tattoo!" He laughed at his own joke as Mr. Kozlowski approached.

"Now see here," said Mr. Kozlowski. "Why are you bothering these men?"

Brian stared at him, dumbstruck. "Men?"

"That's right, men. They work for me. Why don't you leave them alone?"

Brian took a quick look at the older man, dressed in his country clothes, and sized him up. "They're working for you, huh? How much you paying them?"

"Why, that's none of your business."

"You should hire me instead. Those guys are idiots."

"Oh, they are, are they?"

"Yeah, man. I'm smarter than both of those guys put together."

Jeffrey and Pablo watched from inside the garage, too far away to hear the conversation.

"Well, then the timing is perfect," Mr. Kozlowski told Brian. "I'm looking for a smart boy to run an errand for me."

"How much you paying, man?"

Mr. Kozlowski pulled a thick wad of money from the pocket of his overalls. Brian's eyes grew wide at the sight of the bills.

"I'm paying fifty dollars cash," said the older man. "But you've got to get the job done exactly right."

Brian licked his lips. "What do you want me to do?"

"I need you to go to the hardware store on Lankershim Boulevard and pick me up a left-handed monkey wrench."

"A left-handed monkey wrench," Brian repeated, mouthing the words slowly, so as not to forget.

"That's right. I've got plenty of right-handed wrenches, but what I really need is a left-handed one. Now you tell the fellow behind the counter that you're working for me, Mike Kozlowski, and to charge the wrench to my account. Then you bring it back here and I'll pay you fifty dollars."

"I'll go right now," Brian said, turning his bike around.

"The sooner you bring it back, the sooner you get paid."

Brian pedaled off and called over his shoulder. "I'll be back in less than an hour. Have my money ready."

"I sure will," Mr. Kozlowski said, more to himself than Brian. "I sure will." He took a cell phone from his pocket and dialed a number. "Hello, Burt? It's Mike Kozlowski. I've just sent a boy over for a left-handed monkey wrench.... Yeah, that's right. Put it on my account." He chuckled as he clicked the phone off and walked back into the garage.

"What did you tell him?" Pablo asked.

"You'll see, Pablo," the older man replied, with a sly grin on his face. "You'll see."

With Mr. Kozlowski's help, the boys cleaned and polished the musical instruments, and dusted off their cases. Inside one of the cases, Jeffrey found an old dusty trumpet. He had played the trumpet in his sixth grade music class, but that was a cheap, flimsy thing. This one felt heavy and sturdy. As he cleaned it off, he spotted some tiny red specks inside the instrument's bell. He didn't notice them at first, but when he turned the trumpet so that the sunlight hit it, there they were. The specks resembled dried blood.

That's odd, he thought. Why would blood be on a trumpet? He was about to bring it to Mr. Kozlowski's attention, when Pablo shouted, "Hey, Mr. Kozlowski, look at this!" and waved some yellowed newspaper clippings in the air.

Mr. Kozlowski ambled over and Pablo handed him the discovery. Jeffrey put the trumpet back in its case and walked over to join them. Mr. Kozlowski's hands trembled as he looked through the old clippings. "These are from Vietnam," he said quietly.

"The war?" Pablo asked.

The older man nodded.

"Were you in the war, Mr. Kozlowski?" Pablo asked.

"Yes, son, I was." He sat on a bench, the clippings in hand. The boys crowded around him.

"They told us in school that we lost the Vietnam War, but my dad says that's not true," Jeffrey said.

"Your father is right, Jeffrey," Mr. Kozlowski told him. "We fought two wars then, one against the communists of North Vietnam, and another against the protesters here at home. I was nineteen-years-old then, only a few years older than you boys are now, and I was spit on, and called a baby-killer, and a whole slew of other names that would make a truck driver blush. But despite all that, we won the war. The North Vietnamese signed the Paris Peace Accords in 1973 and the war was essentially over. But then a funny thing happened. The politicians in Congress turned their backs on the people of Vietnam. They pulled the funding for our boys and everything began to unravel. I was on one of the last helicopters to leave the Embassy before it fell to the communists."

His voice broke and he took a full minute to regain his composure. The boys watched him intently.

"When the communists saw how Washington betrayed their own military, they began a major offensive. Cambodia fell first in April of 1975, and everyone knew Vietnam was next. We were given a top secret evacuation code: a weather report for Saigon of '105 degrees and rising,' followed by several bars of the song White Christmas, played at fifteen minute intervals over the radio. We knew that when the evacuation code was played, it was the end of the Vietnamese people. Two weeks later, the message was broadcast over the radio."

The older man paused, his eyes glazed over.

"We began pulling out immediately, with helicopter airlifts from the Embassy in Saigon. A great stream of humanity flooded towards us, climbing the Embassy fence and trying to board the helicopters. We knew what would happen to the people when the communists came in, so we took as many as we could, but we couldn't take everyone. There were just too many and we didn't have time. The communist tanks were just outside the city and closing in fast."

He squinted as an image crystallized in his mind.

"I remember the face of a young girl ... a Vietnamese girl, she couldn't have been older than sixteen, with a baby in her arms. She was just one face in a sea of thousands, but she looked directly in my eyes. 'The communists can kill me,' she said, 'but please don't let them kill my baby!' She had tears streaming down her face, and she held her arms out, begging me to take her baby, but I just couldn't. We had no more room on the helicopter. Her face was the last thing I saw before my chopper lifted off."

There was a long moment of silence before Pablo spoke. "Why did the people protest the war, Mr. Kozlowski?"

"Some were misinformed. Others just didn't want to get drafted. But one thing's for sure, when America pulled out of Vietnam, the devil moved in. The communists murdered millions of people. Millions. Men, women, children, babies.... Of course, nobody protested any of that. That young girl with her baby, I'm sure they were murdered, too."

He folded the yellow clippings neatly into quarters and slid them inside his shirt pocket. "You won't hear it from your teachers, or read about it in your school books, boys, but it's all true." He took off his glasses, rubbed his eyes, and stared down at the floor, his mind in a past that lay thousands of miles away.

The boys were silent, each wrapped in his own thoughts. They were no longer children, but neither were they men. They knew that someday they might be called to war, and each boy wondered how he would respond.

Shouts came from outside.

The boys turned their heads. Mr. Kozlowski squinted out at the street and slid his glasses back on.

Brian raced his bicycle into the garage and hopped off, letting his bike fall with a loud clang on the concrete floor. He was sweating profusely, his face and ears were sunburned, and he was swelled up like an angry turkey gobbler.

"Hey, old man!" he shouted. "I went to that hardware store you told me about ... Guy who owns it said they don't have any left-handed monkey wrenches, so he sends me to a store in Reseda, clear across town. I go there, but they don't have any left-handed wrenches, either. They tell me there's a shop in Canoga Park that does. So I go to Canoga Park, but they're sold out! The guy behind the counter says he'll do me a favor, and he calls a place in Studio City. They tell him over the phone that they only have one left, and if I want it I better hurry. So I rush over there as fast as I can, but they tell me I'm five minutes too late! Another guy just bought it! Then I go to the last hardware store I can think of, back here in North Hollywood, and when I ask for a left-handed monkey wrench everyone in the place looks at me and laughs. Turns out there ain't no such thing!"

"Well!" exclaimed Mr. Kozlowski, rising to his feet. "Do you mean to tell me that it took you all this time to figure that out? I thought you said you were smarter than both of these fellas here put together."

"You're a **************!" Brian let loose with a string of bad words and snatched up his bicycle.

"Did your father teach you to talk that way?" Mr. Kozlowski said.

"You're gonna hear from my father!" Brian yelled, as he pedaled away. He made an obscene gesture with his hand and disappeared down the street.

Pablo was smiling. "Mr. Kozlowski, did you send him to get a left-handed monkey wrench?"

"I sure did."

The boys laughed. "Are you scared of his dad coming?" Pablo asked.

"Oh, I might be a little scared," the older man confessed. "But if he tells his father what happened, then he'll have to admit just how big a fool he was, and something tells me he's not the type to do that."

"Oh, no," said Pablo. "Brian never admits to anything, even when he's caught red-handed."

"Well, there you go," said Mr. Kozlowski. He smiled and scratched his head. "Aw, maybe I shouldn't have done it, but I just couldn't resist. Boys, don't ever fall for a left-handed monkey wrench, or you'll be the one who looks like a monkey."

Jeffrey and Pablo laughed.

Chapter 14

Jeffrey and Pablo dismounted their bikes and walked them down the sidewalk. The address to Mr. Weeden's house that Marisol had given them led to this sleepy residential street, lined with elegant houses. Each home had a huge manicured lawn, tended by toiling gardeners. The street was bare, except for a gardener's truck, and the sidewalk was the cleanest either boy had ever seen. There was no sound, save for chirping birds and a pair of lawnmower engines, and even the lawnmowers seemed to operate in hushed tones. The boys felt far removed from the rest of the city and their own neighborhood.

They stopped for a moment to watch a gardener in a cowboy hat, his face darkened and lined from years in the sun, run a lawnmower over an especially beautiful lawn. It reminded Pablo of the summers when he helped his uncle mow lawns. He was a small boy then, and his job was to empty the grass bag from the lawnmower. Pablo never forgot the smell of freshly cut grass that filled his nostrils when he emptied the bag.

They continued down the sidewalk until they reached the address Marisol had given them. It was a large, stately house, like the others, with a perfectly kept lawn and a babbling fountain in the front yard. "Pretty big house for a guy who owns a pawn shop," Pablo said.

Jeffrey nodded. "I was just thinking the same thing."

Across the street, they saw an elderly man on his knees in his front yard, pruning rose bushes. The man wore faded denim overalls, thick-lensed glasses, and a wide-brimmed hat.

The boys crossed the street, laid their bicycles down on the sidewalk, and approached him. The man saw them coming and offered a wide, toothy grin.

"Hello, boys," the man said. He seemed happy to have company. Pablo wondered if the man was lonely and lived by himself in the big house. He smiled back.

"Hello, sir," Jeffrey said. "Are you Mr. Smithers?"

The man laid his gardening shears down on the lawn and looked at them with wonder. "Now how did you know that?"

Jeffrey handed the man their business card. The man read the card and shook his head. "Well, you certainly are fine detectives."

Jeffrey pulled out a pen and his notes. "If we may, sir, we'd like to ask you a couple of questions about the painting that was stolen from Mr. Weeden's house last week. We understand you saw someone leaving the house with the painting."

"Yes, that's true. I was right here, as a matter of fact, right in this very spot, and I looked up and I saw a young man with long hair coming out of Mr. Weeden's garage." He pointed across the street to Mr. Weeden's house. Jeffrey and Pablo turned and followed the man's line of sight.

"The young man carried a large painting, and I thought to myself, 'That's rather odd.' Then he got on a bicycle, and with one hand on the handlebars, and the other hand holding the painting, he rode off down the street."

"Did the police show you a photograph of the suspect?" Jeffrey asked.

"They showed me several photographs and I picked one. Now mind you, I wasn't one hundred percent sure, but I picked the one that I thought most resembled the young man that I saw."

Jeffrey thanked the man, then he and Pablo walked slowly back to their bikes.

"Good luck with your investigation, boys!" Mr. Smithers called after them.

When they reached the sidewalk, Jeffrey turned and gave Mr. Smithers a thumbs-up sign.

"What are you doing?" Pablo whispered.

"Testing his eyesight," Jeffrey whispered in response.

Mr. Smithers grinned and gave them a thumbs-up sign back.

"He passed," Jeffrey said.

Chapter 15

The overhead sun pressed down its heat as Jeffrey and Pablo rode their bikes home. If they kept moving, a slight breeze fluttered their shirts. But at every stop, their clammy, sweat-soaked clothes would suck in and cling to their bodies. Neither boy spoke. They both knew that if a witness had identified Victor with the painting, then he had to be guilty.

Jeffrey suggested they each do independent research and then meet later that night. Pablo went to the library to use the computer. He looked up websites for both Mr. Weeden's business and the tattoo shop, and he searched the internet for information on thefts of valuable paintings. He made notes on everything he read, including some facts that he knew Jeffrey would find interesting.

Jeffrey used his mother's computer and did some research of his own. That night, in Jeffrey's basement, he and Pablo went over the case.

"The owner of the tattoo shop is Bob Sullivan," Pablo began, reading from his notes. "He's been in business for ten years, and he has a lot of celebrity clients. A lot of actors, like Brittany James, plus musicians, singers, comics, and a bunch of wannabe celebrities, like kids of rich and famous people. Now Mr. Weeden told us that when Bob Sullivan first brought the painting in he said he was behind in his rent. But if he has all these celebrity clients, paying for expensive tattoos, then that doesn't make any sense. I think either Bob Sullivan was lying to Mr. Weeden, or Mr. Weeden was lying to us."

"Good point, Pablo." Jeffrey said. "And good deduction. Continue."

"Mr. Weeden has been in business over twenty years. Everything Mr. Kozlowski told us about him is true. Twenty years ago, when his shop was still downtown, there was a suspicious fire in his building. The fire investigators suspected arson, but they could never prove it, and Mr. Weeden collected a large insurance settlement. There was a second fire in another downtown building about ten years ago, and again he collected a big insurance settlement. After the second fire, Mr. Weeden reopened his pawn shop in North Hollywood. Now here's something interesting ..."

He paused for dramatic effect and Jeffrey listened.

"There was a handyman that worked for Mr. Weeden named Sam Britts. He was arrested for starting the fire, but eventually the police let him go. The handyman insisted he was innocent and that Mr. Weeden had framed him, but that was never proven."

Jeffrey sat straight up. "We have to question that handyman."

"That won't be easy," Pablo said.

"Why not?"

"He's dead."

Jeffrey's eyes opened wide. Pablo continued. "He was murdered two days after the police let him out of jail. Someone hit him over the head. The police questioned Mr. Weeden about that, too."

"This Mr. Weeden is a very suspicious character," Jeffrey observed.

"The handyman, Sam Britts, was actually Vietnamese," Pablo said. "He was airlifted out of Saigon when he was six-years-old on one of the helicopters Mr. Kozlowski told us about. I can't pronounce his Vietnamese name. Sam Britts is the name he took after being adopted by an American family. Who knows? Maybe he was on the same helicopter as Mr. Kozlowski all those years ago."

"Was Mr. Weeden arrested?" Jeffrey asked.

"No, just questioned. The murder was never solved."

"This Weeden gets questioned a lot, but nothing ever sticks."

"Right," said Pablo. "Two unsolved fires and an unsolved murder. If he did burn his own building down and tried to blame it on Sam Britts, then it's possible that he also stole his own painting and is trying to blame it on Victor."

"Another good deduction," Jeffrey said.

Pablo continued his report. "Very few stolen paintings are ever recovered, less than ten percent. Most of the thefts are burglaries and the police don't pay them much attention. However, the F.B.I. has its own Art Crime Team.

"The problem with stealing a valuable painting is they're hard to sell. The only people who buy stolen paintings are private collectors who are rich enough to afford them, and then they have to hide the painting someplace where no one else can see it, which sounds pretty stupid to me. So what happens with most stolen paintings is they're ransomed back to their owners or to the insurance companies so they don't have to pay a settlement. It's called art-napping." He lowered his notes. "That's all."

"Excellent work, Pablo. Excellent."

Pablo smiled wide.

Jeffrey reached for his own notes. "I used my mom's computer to print out a copy of the painting, 'Flowers of Spain' by Frances Columbus." He showed Pablo a colorful picture of a Spanish field, covered with red carnations, Spanish bluebells, and Valencia roses.

Pablo studied the picture with its rich vibrant colors. "So that's what we're all looking for," he said with awe in his voice.

"I looked all over the internet for an owner's name," Jeffrey said, "but all I could find was that it most likely belonged to a private owner. Now does that look like the kind of painting a guy like Bob Sullivan would be interested in?"

Pablo thought it over. "Well, he did know a lot about art when you talked to him, but no, it doesn't look like the type of painting a guy who owns a tattoo parlor would have. Not a bunch of flowers."

"I agree," Jeffrey said, "and it leads me to deduce that there's only one possible reason why Bob Sullivan took that painting to Mr. Weeden's pawn shop." He paused and Pablo leaned forward, waiting.

"To hide it."

"To hide it?"

"Of course! Think about it. Why would somebody take a painting worth half-a-million dollars to a pawn shop? Bob Sullivan is an expert on art, we know that from talking with him. He knew how much that painting was worth. If he really needed the money, which your research shows is doubtful, he'd sell it to a museum, or a private collector. He wouldn't pawn it. Plus, remember what Mr. Weeden said: Bob Sullivan kept coming back to the pawn shop to check on the painting, like he knew something was wrong. Put all that together and the only logical deduction is that Bob Sullivan needed to hide the painting someplace other than his house or the pawn shop."

"But why would he hide it?" Pablo asked.

"My guess is the painting was stolen. He had to hide it, because he was afraid the police might search his house or his shop."

"Stolen before it was stolen?"

"Exactly. And if he can't keep it at home or at his tattoo shop, then where else can he hide it? It's too big for a safe deposit box. A pawn shop is the perfect place to hide a stolen painting."

Pablo leapt to his feet. "That means Victor is innocent!"

"Not necessarily," Jeffrey said. "I did some research on Mr. Smithers. He's a retired architect with a long history of charity work. And he has good eyesight, as we tested. As a witness, he's solid as a rock. If he saw Victor leaving Mr. Weeden's house with the painting, then our chances of proving that Victor is innocent are pretty slim. If we can't solve that, then we'll have to concede that Victor is guilty. As you brought up, it's possible that Victor stole a painting that was already stolen."

Pablo paced the room. "You've always told me that the first step in any investigation is to eliminate the impossible."

Jeffrey nodded. "That's right."

"Mr. Weeden told us there was no sign of a break-in at his house, and that the only thing that was stolen was the painting. So whoever took it must have known that it was there."

"I agree. Go on."

"If Victor and Laura broke up two weeks ago, then I think we can eliminate her from the list of people who knew about the painting. That leaves only four possible suspects: Victor, Bob Sullivan, Eddie, and Mr. Weeden himself. As far as we know, they're the only ones who knew Mr. Weeden had the painting. Let's go over them one by one and see if we can figure out who the thief is."

"Excellent idea," Jeffrey said. "Let's start with Bob Sullivan."

The boys went over each suspect. They talked and talked, and always it came back to the same conclusion: The witness, Mr. Smithers, who saw Victor leaving the scene of the crime with the painting. There was just no way of getting around it.

Finally, Pablo yawned and said, "All this thinking is making my brain tired."

"Me, too," Jeffrey agreed. "It's late. Let's call it a night and reconvene in the morning."

Pablo stood up and stretched. "What about the witness? Do we mention him to Marisol?"

Jeffrey frowned. "Not yet. If Victor really is guilty, it's going to crush her."

Chapter 16

Pablo took one step out of Jeffrey's air-conditioned house and his shirt was already soaked with sweat. As he walked his bike down Jeffrey's driveway, he heard a faint whimper. He turned and saw Marisol, sitting alone in her pajamas on her front porch, quietly weeping. She was perspiring from the heat and her hair lay damp and tousled across her forehead and shoulders.

Pablo laid his bike down on the grass, walked over, and sat next to her. "You okay?" he asked.

Marisol nodded. "We went to see Victor in jail today. He looked so skinny and frightened. He said he lost weight, because they have so little food, and he had a big purple bruise on his cheek from a fight."

Pablo winced. Marisol sniffled and wiped her eyes.

"When we were little, Victor always watched over me. He was super protective. He used to walk me to kindergarten and to first grade. And he was funny, too. When my mom would have a party at night, she'd put us to bed, so the lights in our room would be out, but we could hear music playing from the living room. We'd jump up and down on our beds in the dark and dance to the music. Then Victor would pretend to sing. He was so silly."

She tried to smile and shook her head. "I'm so scared for Victor. I know he's innocent, but I can't get him out of jail!" The tears began to flow again and she hid her face in her hands.

Pablo told her about their visit to the bowling alley. Then he told Marisol something that Jeffrey had often told him. "We're investigators. We have intelligence and we know how to reason. If there's a way to solve this mystery, we will."

Marisol wiped her face with her sleeve. "Thank you, Pablo," she whispered.

For a long time, they sat and said nothing. The night was still, save for a barking dog and the lonely call of a distant train whistle. Marisol leaned her head gently on his shoulder. She was almost asleep. Pablo was wide awake. He wondered what would become of her if Victor was found guilty and sentenced to a long time in jail.

The girl's breathing was slow and rhythmic. He glanced down carefully so as not to wake her. Nestled against him, with her eyes closed and the moonlight reflecting off her hair, she looked to Pablo like the prettiest girl he'd ever seen.

Behind them a clatter came from the house. "Marisol? Marisol, where are you?" It was the sleepy voice of Mrs. Rodriguez.

Marisol stirred and laid a small hand on Pablo's shoulder. He felt her warm breath on his ear as she whispered, "Goodnight, Pablo."

Then she was up and gone, the screen door flapping closed behind her.

Chapter 17

Jeffrey was sound asleep at seven o'clock in the morning when the phone rang. In the dark contours of the basement, the ring sounded like a high-pitched scream, ricocheting off the walls and jarring him awake.

A moment ago, he'd been oblivious to the world, his face buried in soft pillows, dreaming away. Now he couldn't even remember what his dream was about, only that it left him with a vague sense of sadness. He tried bringing the dream back into focus, but what had seemed so real and vivid only seconds ago, was now a hazy memory, slipping and swaying and rolling away ...

RRING!

There it was again. Jeffrey reached for his glasses on the nightstand table. Fumbling and mumbling, he leaned out of bed and picked up the phone on the third ring. "Hello?"

"Hello, this is Steven Smithers," said the voice on the line. "I believe we spoke yesterday."

"Oh yeah, Mr. Smithers. This is Jeffrey Jones."

"I hope I didn't wake you."

"No, it's okay," Jeffrey said, trying to sound more alert. "I had to get up anyway."

"Well, I found your number on the business card you gave me, so I called because there's something I want to tell you. After you boys left yesterday, I got to thinking about our conversation, and I realized there was something I forgot to mention. I don't even know if I mentioned it to the police or if it's worth mentioning to you. It seemed so unimportant at the time, but just the same, I thought you might like to know."

"Yes, sir, I'm listening," Jeffrey said, wide awake now.

"Well, what I thought you might want to know is that when I saw the boy on his bicycle with the painting, I also saw a girl. Not at the same time, but a few minutes later."

Jeffrey reached for a pen and paper. "Tell me what happened, sir."

"Well, I was still working in my yard, as I told you, and I looked up and I saw a girl walking down Joe Weeden's driveway."

"Do you remember what she looked like, Mr. Smithers?"

"As I recall, she was young, about eighteen-years-old. Blond hair.... Nice looking girl."

"And then what happened?"

"Well, that's it. I saw her for a few seconds, and then I went back to my roses. I had completely forgotten about it until you boys stopped by and I started to think more about that day."

Jeffrey's mind was racing. Was Laura the girl Mr. Smithers had seen? "If you saw a picture of the girl, do you think you would recognize her?"

"Maybe I could. I really don't know."

"Are you going to be home today, sir?"

"Sure. Do you boys want to stop by?"

"Definitely. Give me a few hours."

"I'll be here."

"Thank you, sir."

Jeffrey waited an hour, to give Pablo time to wake up, then called his friend and told him about his phone conversation with Mr. Smithers. Fifteen minutes later, the boys were meeting in Jeffrey's basement.

"I've had a suspicion since we first talked to Laura, that she was somehow mixed up in this," Jeffrey said. "Or, at the very least, that she's hiding something. If we can get a picture of her to show Mr. Smithers, we can ask him if she's the same girl he saw on Mr. Weeden's driveway the day the painting was stolen."

"Sounds good," said Pablo, "but how do we get a picture of Laura?"

"Well, we have two options. We can borrow someone's phone and try taking her picture at the bowling alley when she's not looking. The risk to that idea is she might see us and that could create a problem. Plus, whoever's phone we borrow is going to want to come along, and that could create a problem, too. We'd either have to lie, or tell them about our case, and right now, I think it's better if we keep our investigation between the two of us, and between Marisol, who already knows."

"I think so, too," Pablo said. "What's the second option?"

"The second option is to ask Marisol if she can find a picture of Laura on Victor's cell phone, or somewhere in his room. The problem with that option is she's going to want to know why we want the picture. We either have to lie, or we have to tell her about Mr. Smithers and how he saw Victor with the painting. I don't know how she'll take that news. It could kill her."

Both boys were silent for a moment, before Jeffrey continued. "Then again, if the case goes to trial, she's going to find out anyway. Maybe it's better if she hears it from us. It's your call, Pablo."

Pablo nodded. He knew Marisol was under a lot of emotional strain and he didn't want to add to it. Still, everything Jeffrey said made sense.

"Let's try option two," he said.

Chapter 18

"He saw Victor with the painting?"

Marisol stared back at Jeffrey and Pablo, her lower lip quivering. "But how could he see Victor with the painting if Victor never took it?"

Pablo glanced at his friend, but Jeffrey kept his eyes locked on Marisol. They were in her house, sitting at the kitchen table. "We haven't solved that yet," Jeffrey said.

"He says he saw a girl leaving Mr. Weeden's house, a few minutes after he saw Victor," Pablo said. "A blond girl that we think might be Laura. We were hoping you had a picture of her that we could show him. We don't know what her connection to this is, but if he did see Laura, it might help us solve the case."

Marisol stared down at the table. "The police took Victor's phone," she said softly. "I'll look in his room. Maybe I can find something." She pushed off from the table and walked out.

Pablo turned to Jeffrey and whispered, "Did we do the right thing?"

Jeffrey nodded and they waited in silence.

Minutes passed and then they heard Marisol's shout, "I got it." She returned to the kitchen with a four by six photograph in her hand. She handed the photo to the boys, sat at the table, and watched as they examined it. The photograph showed Laura, seated at a table and wearing her red work shirt. It looked like it was taken at the refreshment area of the bowling alley.

"Do you think that's the girl Mr. Smithers saw?" Pablo asked Jeffrey, as they studied the photo.

"Only one way to find out," Jeffrey replied. "Let's go show it to him right now."

The boys rose and started for the door.

Marisol stood straight up. "I want to go with you."

The boys stopped and looked at her. Marisol's eyes were determined, but looked ready to spill tears.

Jeffrey shrugged. "Why not? Maybe three heads are better than two."

"Come in, come in, I've been waiting for you," Mr. Smithers said, opening the front door.

Marisol and the boys filed inside and Mr. Smithers led them to his living room and invited them to sit. It was an elegant room with fine furniture and decorated with plants and roses. Marisol and the boys sat together on the sofa.

"Now I would be remiss if I didn't offer you some cool water to drink," the older man said. He went to the kitchen and returned with three bottles of cold water. Passing them out, he nodded at Marisol. "Looks like you have a new partner."

Jeffrey took a deep breath. "This is Marisol Rodriguez. She's the sister of Victor Rodriguez, the guy who was arrested for stealing the painting."

Color drained from the older man's face. "Oh, my ... I'm afraid this is a bit awkward."

"We think Victor is innocent," Jeffrey continued. "But we haven't been able to prove it."

Mr. Smithers sat in a chair and faced them with a pained expression. "I see. Why, I'd feel terrible if I helped to send an innocent boy to jail." He turned to Marisol and looked her directly in the eye. "Please understand that."

"I do," Marisol said.

"It's not your fault, sir," Jeffrey said. "You saw what you saw and reported it to the police. You did the right thing. Maybe with your help we can solve the mystery and discover if someone else is responsible for the crime."

"I'll do whatever I can to help."

Jeffrey pulled out a pen and his notes. "You said on the phone that you saw a boy leaving Mr. Weeden's house with a painting under his arm, and shortly after that you saw a girl leaving the same house."

"Yes, that's true. A blond girl ... about eighteen-years-old.... She was walking down the driveway."

Jeffrey handed Mr. Smithers the picture of Laura. "Does this look like the girl that you saw?"

Mr. Smithers studied the photo. "Yes ... possibly ... that could be her. There's a resemblance, but I can't say that I'm one hundred percent sure. Of course, like I told you before, I wasn't a hundred percent sure about the boy with the painting, either. I told the police that."

"We understand," said Jeffrey. "On a scale of zero to one hundred, what percentage would you estimate that the girl in the photo is the same girl that you saw?"

"Now you're putting me on the spot." He looked more closely at the photo. "Actually, this red shirt ..." He tapped the photo.

Jeffrey perked up. "Yes?"

"I remember that the girl that I saw was wearing a red shirt. Sounds silly, I know. But I remember thinking how the color of her shirt matched the color of my roses. When you work with flowers, you become very sensitive to colors, you know."

"We understand," Jeffrey said. "That makes sense. Do you think the girl in the photo is wearing the same shirt as the girl you saw?"

"I can't say it's the same shirt, but it's the same *color* shirt."

"Back to our question: On a scale of zero to one hundred, what percentage would you estimate that the girl in the photo is the same girl you saw walking down Mr. Weeden's driveway?"

"I'm sixty percent sure it's the same girl, but I'm one hundred percent sure that the girl I saw was wearing a shirt the same color as this shirt in your picture." He handed the photo back to Jeffrey. "Now I insist that you keep me informed about your investigation. Promise me you'll let me know how it all turns out."

"I promise, sir," Jeffrey said. "You'll be the first person I call once the mystery is solved."

Mr. Smithers turned to Marisol. "Miss, if your brother is innocent, then I am truly sorry. I only told the police what I saw."

"I understand," Marisol said. "Thank you."

Chapter 19

It was a strange bike ride home. Marisol's hands trembled as they gripped her handlebars, still shaken over the news that a witness had actually seen Victor with the painting.

Jeffrey pumped his legs furiously, excited about the possible clue that Mr. Smithers had given them regarding Laura. *If she was the one Mr. Smithers had seen on Mr. Weeden's driveway ...?*

Pablo kept an eye on both of them. He felt both sad for Marisol and excited for Jeffrey, and he wondered if something was wrong with him.

None of them spoke and when they arrived home, Marisol went straight inside her house without a word. Jeffrey and Pablo took a short walk to the ice cream shop on the corner. It was an old-fashioned shop from the fifties, with a ceiling fan, wooden tables covered with red and white checkered tablecloths, and even a little bell over the door that tinkled when someone came in or out.

As Jeffrey and Pablo stepped inside, there were two girls, shorter than them, but the same age, already at the counter. One girl had dark hair and was wearing glasses and a hat. The other girl had red wavy hair.

The girls ordered their ice cream and turned around. The dark-haired girl looked at Jeffrey. Jeffrey looked at the dark-haired girl. They both said, "Oh, no!"

"What are you doing here?" the girl demanded.

"What are *you* doing here?" Jeffrey demanded back.

"I asked you first. Following us, no doubt!"

Jeffrey groaned, upset with himself for not recognizing Susie Norris when they first walked in. She wore the same owl-shaped glasses as Jeffrey and had the same inquisitive face. She was wearing a felt fedora with a feather in it, the silliest hat Jeffrey had ever seen. Now she was going to ruin his ice cream.

Susie turned to Pablo with a wide smile. "How goes it, Pablo?"

"Hi, Susie."

Susie put her arm around the red-haired girl's shoulder. "Pablo, this is my friend, Gina."

Gina smiled, revealing a mouthful of metal and dimples on her cheeks. She and Pablo exchanged greetings. Then with a sigh and a dramatic wave of her arm, Susie said, "And this is Jeffrey Jones."

"Hi, Jeffrey!" Gina said.

"Hey," Jeffrey muttered, offering not the slightest bit of enthusiasm.

"As you can see, he's a social wiz," Susie said.

The teenage clerk behind the counter handed Susie and Gina each a double-scooped cone of strawberry ice cream. The girls stepped back and the boys stepped up to the counter.

Susie licked her ice cream. "So what's up, Pablo? What have you and Mr. Jones been up to?"

"We started a detective club. We're working on a case. A mystery."

"Oh, tell me! Tell me!"

"We can't tell you, it's confidential," Jeffrey said.

"Confidential for who?"

"For all parties involved."

"Does that include me?"

Jeffrey ignored her and ordered his ice cream. Susie whispered to Pablo, "Come on, Pablo. You can tell me!"

Jeffrey spun on his heel. "It's a mystery! We can't tell anyone!"

Susie poked Jeffrey in the stomach with her index finger. "The only mystery I can see is why you don't go on a diet."

Jeffrey turned back to face the counter, his face flaming red. Susie stepped around to his side and spoke to his profile. "As it just so happens, Mr. Jones, I believe I have some information about your case."

"Like what?"

"Like I'm not going to tell you." She turned away and took a defiant lick of her ice cream.

"You don't know anything about our case," Pablo said. "You don't even know what our case is."

"That's what you think, mister."

"If you knew anything about our case, you'd tell us," Jeffrey insisted, a little too loud, and a little too angry. Now he wasn't just mad at Susie, he was mad at himself. It wasn't like him to lose his composure.

"I was going to tell you," Susie said, "but just for that, I'm not. Come on, Gina. Let's leave these country peasants. Not you, Pablo."

The girls turned up their noses and marched for the door.

"What do you think she knows?" Pablo whispered.

"Nothing," Jeffrey said firmly. "She knows nothing." The clerk handed him an ice cream cone and Jeffrey snapped at it like an attack dog.

The girls paused dramatically in the doorway and locked arms. "We're leaving now!" Susie called. Jeffrey refused to look.

The girls stepped outside and crossed the parking lot, arm-in-arm. "What are they doing?" Susie whispered.

Gina glanced back over her shoulder. "Nothing.... No, wait ... Pablo's looking at us."

"Quick, turn around!" Susie said.

Inside the shop, Jeffrey and Pablo took a seat at a table. "Are you sure she doesn't know anything?" Pablo said. "She seemed pretty sure of herself."

"She's always sure of herself. That's her problem. Her ego is bigger than her brain." Jeffrey bit at his ice cream.

"I hate to think we'd overlooked a clue," Pablo said. "Susie is pretty smart. And you always tell me that an investigator has to follow every lead. Isn't that what you always tell me?"

Jeffrey grunted. He looked out the window at the two girls as they grew smaller in the distance. What if Susie did know something about their case? What if she knew something and he let her go without questioning her? "Come on," he said, and the two boys rushed outside.

"Wait!" Jeffrey called across the parking lot. The girls pretended they didn't hear him and kept on walking.

"Susie, wait!" Jeffrey called again. The girls stopped and turned around. Jeffrey and Pablo ran across the parking lot and caught up with them.

"What do you know about our case?" Jeffrey demanded.

"Why should I tell you?"

"Come on, Susie," Pablo insisted. "A friend of ours is in jail and we're trying to help him!"

"Who's your friend? Do I know him?"

"Never mind," said Jeffrey. "Just tell us what you know. This is serious."

Gina gave Susie a nudge. Susie nudged her back, and faced the boys. "Well, what I was going to tell you is my mom was driving me home the other night, and we heard a bunch of loud bangs, like explosions, by your house. We thought they were gunshots, but then we saw some guy throwing firecrackers out of a car in front of your house. I tried to take a picture with my phone, but the car drove away too fast."

"Who was it?" Jeffrey asked.

"I don't know. I couldn't see the driver. The guy throwing the firecrackers was on the passenger side and I couldn't see him that well."

"What kind of car was it?"

"I don't know that, either. It was dark and I don't know cars very well. I think it was red."

"What else?"

"What do you mean 'what else'?"

"What else do you know?"

"That's it."

"That's it? That's all you know? That's no help!"

"Well, what do you expect? You want me to solve your whole case? I mean, I could if I wanted to, but that's not the point."

Jeffrey threw up his hands. "This is a waste of time!" He turned and headed back for the ice cream shop. Pablo followed him.

Susie called after them. "Don't I get a thank you?"

"Thanks for nothing!" Jeffrey called back, without turning around.

"That's gratitude! Maybe I'll start my own detective club!"

"Go ahead!"

"ARRR!" Susie growled to Gina. "That Jeffrey Jones is a public nuisance!"

Back in the ice cream shop, Jeffrey and Pablo sat at a table and finished their ice cream. Jeffrey stared out the window with a faraway look in his eye.

"Are you thinking what I'm thinking?" Pablo asked.

Jeffrey blinked. "About the car?"

"Yeah, remember who we saw driving a red car to the tattoo shop? Brittany James."

Jeffrey nodded. "That's what I was thinking. But I don't see how it's possible. Why would someone famous like that be throwing firecrackers at my house? She doesn't know me. She doesn't know where I live. The only ones who saw our business card are Mr. Weeden, Eddie, and Mr. Smithers."

"And we didn't see Mr. Smithers until after the firecrackers."

"Right. The odds that the car Susie saw belongs to Brittany James are a million-to-one."

"Well, even at a million-to-one, it's still a lead."

"True."

"And right now the only leads we have are the blond girl that Mr. Smithers saw and Susie's red car."

Jeffrey sighed. "True."

"So do we investigate it? The car, I mean?"

"I guess we have to."

"What if Susie's lead turns into something? Are you going to apologize to her?"

Jeffrey pondered Pablo's question as if the survival of the free world depended upon his answer. "Apologizing to Susie Norris," he finally decided, "would be a fate worse than death."

Chapter 20

Saturday morning found Jeffrey and Pablo doing the same thing they'd done every Saturday morning since the fifth grade: helping Father Pat who ran the church mission.

There were piles of donated clothes to wash, dry, and iron; bags of toothpaste, soap, and other essentials to sort through; and hundreds of cans of soup, vegetables, and sliced peaches to count, stack, and pack.

Most of the goods went overseas to various church missions, but some was distributed locally. Jeffrey and Pablo had even accompanied Father Pat on a trip to downtown's skid row to help pass out blankets and food. It was an eye-opener for the boys and they had talked about it for weeks afterwards.

Sometimes other volunteers were there at the church to help, and sometimes Jeffrey and Pablo were alone and did all the work themselves. Either way, they never missed a Saturday. They liked knowing they were helping to feed and clothe the poor, and they liked spending time with Father Pat.

"Oh, I'm going to miss you boys when high school starts," the priest often said.

"We'll still be around," Pablo would reply.

"Well, I hope so. I know you'll be plenty busy with football games, school activities, and homework."

Father Pat had white hair and a kind face. Of all the teachers at St. Mary's Middle School, he was the one who encouraged them the most. He gave them literary classics to read, like Shakespeare, Mark Twain, and *Johnny Tremain* by Esther Forbes; and their time together on Saturday mornings was often spent discussing art, literature, history, religion, and life.

On this Saturday, Jeffrey and Pablo were alone in the church basement, opening boxes. Budget cuts had forced a neighboring school in the district to abandon their baseball and theater programs, so they'd donated all their old uniforms, theater costumes, and baseball equipment to the mission.

The boys were cutting open the boxes and sorting through their contents. Pablo had just discovered a perfectly broken-in baseball mitt when Father Pat descended the stairs.

"Check this out, Father!"

Pablo tossed him the mitt. Father Pat caught it and slipped the soft leather glove over his left hand. He stretched his fingers inside the mitt and smacked the glove's palm with the heel of his right hand.

"Now this is what I call a baseball mitt," Father Pat said. "I've seen some fine mitts in my day, but this one takes the cake. Whoever gets this glove is sure going to be happy. Maybe we should wait until Christmas and give it away then."

"But it's summer now," Pablo said. "Someone could use it to play baseball now."

"Pablo, when you're right, you're right. And you're right," said Father Pat. He handed the glove back to the boy. "How about you, Jeffrey...? Find anything good?"

"I always find good stuff, Father," Jeffrey said, digging through a box of theater costumes. "How about this...?" He slipped a monocle over his eye and put a top hat on his head. Pablo and Father Pat both laughed.

Father Pat tapped his chin with his index finger. "You know, there was something here that reminded me of you, Jeffrey. Now where was it?" He poked around the boxes and stopped at one labeled COSTUMES. "Ah, try this on for size."

He reached into the box and pulled out a Sherlock Holmes deerstalker cap and a 19th century pipe. With a sly smile on his face, he handed the items to Jeffrey.

Jeffrey put the cap on his head, held the pipe close to his mouth, and with an impeccable English accent he said, "The game's afoot, Watson!"

Laughter from Pablo and Father Pat bounced off the walls. Pablo laughed so hard he nearly fell on the floor. Father Pat laughed so hard he had to wipe tears from his eyes.

Each time their laughter would start to die down, Jeffrey, with the cap still on his head and the pipe in his hand, would declare, in perfectly accented English, "Moriarty, you fiend!" or "You know my methods, Watson!" and the howls of laughter would burst forth again. Pablo would be nearly on the floor, and Father Pat would grip his aching side and shout, "You're killing me, Jeffrey! You're killing me!"

To which Jeffrey would reply, "What? Ho, Watson! Away with you!" and Pablo and Father Pat would laugh even harder.

It was a good fifteen minutes before they returned to any semblance of normal.

"Jeffrey, tell Father Pat about our club!" Pablo cried, still laughing.

"Your club...?" Father Pat asked, wiping his eyes with a handkerchief.

"We started a club," Pablo said. "A detective club.... Tell him, Jeffrey."

"We started a detective club, Father, like Pablo said, and we're working on our first case. Victor Rodriguez was arrested for stealing a painting and we're trying to prove he's innocent."

Father Pat froze and stared back at him. "Victor Rodriguez was arrested?"

Victor had been a student at St. Mary's and Father Pat knew him well. All the joy that was in the priest's face a moment ago drained away, and he suddenly looked very old.

Jeffrey and Pablo glanced at each other, and wished they'd kept quiet. They were too young to understand all the trials and disappointments of a religious life, but old enough to know that a priest's life is filled more with sorrow than joy. They knew that Father Pat's heart had been broken a hundred times before by the bright young children of St. Mary's, their faces filled with wonder and promise, only to end up in gangs, in prison, or dead.

"I'm sorry, Father," Jeffrey said. He put the pipe down and removed the deerstalker cap.

Pablo looked away and muttered, "Sorry, Father."

"No, no. It's good that you told me. I wouldn't have known otherwise. Tell me more."

The boys told him about their investigation and everyone they'd talked to. Father Pat nodded his head gravely as they spoke. When they'd finished, the priest steadied himself, but his voice was shaky. "I know Victor had some trouble in high school, but I thought he'd grown beyond that. He was attending church regularly. I saw him most every Sunday. This doesn't sound like him at all."

"That's what we think, Father," Jeffrey said, trying to sound optimistic. "We just don't have enough evidence at this point to prove it."

Father Pat breathed a lonely sigh. "Well, I hope your investigation bears fruit. If anyone can do it, it's you, Jeffrey. And you, Pablo." He gave them each a pat on the shoulder. "Excuse me, boys."

Jeffrey and Pablo watched as the frail, white-haired priest climbed the basement stairs, his back hunched with the weight of a thousand broken dreams.

The two boys finished the morning's work in silence.

Chapter 21

"Trash goes out on Monday."

"I know, Dad."

"Feed the fish twice a day."

"I know, Mom."

"The phone number to the hotel is on the refrigerator and on your mother's desk."

"I know, Dad. I know. We've been over this a hundred times."

"Then we'll go over it a hundred and one times."

"Jeffrey," his mother said, "there's plenty of food in the kitchen to last you until we return, but you'll have to make it yourself. Be careful with the stove. Don't burn anything. Don't burn the house down."

Jeffrey rolled his eyes.

"Don't roll your eyes at me! I'm serious."

"You can go to church on Sunday," his father said, "and hang out with Pablo on Monday, but that's it. I don't want you leaving the house for any reason unless it's an emergency. Understand?"

"I understand."

"Good. Mr. Kozlowski gave you a couple of days off so there's no need for you to go anywhere."

"Don't worry," Jeffrey said. "I'll stay here in my prison cell."

His mother snapped, "That's enough, Jeffrey!"

"You don't have to treat me like a little kid," Jeffrey protested. "I'm not an idiot."

His parents looked at each other. "Nobody's accusing you of being an idiot, Jeffrey," his father said. "We're just concerned. We're leaving you on your own for a couple of days. Don't let us down."

"I won't."

"One more thing: I don't want anyone except Pablo, and maybe this girl Marisol, in the house. No one else, understand? I don't want any wild parties going on in here while we're gone."

Jeffrey nodded. He didn't bother telling his father that if he threw a party, no one but Pablo would bother showing up.

"Alright, son.... Good luck. We're counting on you." Jeffrey's father extended his hand. Surprised, Jeffrey took his father's hand and they shook. Then his mother kissed his cheek, gave him a pat on the shoulder, and they were gone.

He watched out the living room window as the family car backed out of the driveway, honked twice, and then drove off down the street, disappearing around the corner.

Suddenly, the house was silent, save for the bubbling of the aquarium behind him.

He was on his own.

Chapter 22

"You guys go downstairs, I'll be down in a minute," Jeffrey said, as he swung the front door open. Pablo and Marisol stepped inside and clattered down the basement steps.

Jeffrey went to his mother's computer and searched for images of Brittany James. He found one of her standing beside a red sports car and printed a color copy. With a pair of scissors, he carefully cut Brittany James out of the picture.

Then he went in the kitchen, where a sheet of paper was attached by a magnet to the refrigerator door. On the paper was a list of emergency phone numbers – Police, Fire, Hospital – and underneath those was a list of phone numbers belonging to relatives and friends.

Jeffrey knew that his mother was an acquaintance of Susie's mother, and he thought their phone number was probably somewhere on the list. He scrolled his finger down the column of phone numbers and saw that he was right. He wrote the number down on a slip of paper. Then he took both Susie's phone number and the picture he printed of Brittany James's car, and ran downstairs.

Pablo and Marisol were seated together on the small sofa. Pablo was telling her about their conversation with Susie at the ice cream shop.

"Pablo, check this out," Jeffrey said. He handed Pablo the picture he had printed out, and took a seat on his beanbag chair.

Marisol leaned over Pablo's arm to look. "What's this?" she asked.

"It's Brittany James's car," Jeffrey said.

Pablo studied the picture. "This looks like the car we saw at the tattoo shop. Do you think it's the same car Susie saw?"

"We can find out. Why don't you call her and arrange to meet. You can show her that picture and ask her if it's the same car."

"Oh, no," Pablo insisted. "I'm not calling her!" He shoved the picture back at Jeffrey.

"Come on, Pablo!"

"No way, man."

"It's for our case, our investigation...."

"You're the senior detective," Pablo said. "It's your job to call her."

"I think you should call her, Jeffrey," Marisol said.

"Who asked you?"

"I'm an impartial observer."

Jeffrey groaned.

"I know Susie from school," Marisol said. "She's not going to bite you."

"Come on, senior detective!" Pablo said. "It's just a phone call."

"Do you have Susie's phone number?" Marisol asked.

Jeffrey held up the slip of paper with Susie's number. "My mom knows her mom," he explained.

"Then call her!" Marisol pleaded. "Please, Jeffrey! Do it for me!"

"Can you call her, Marisol?"

"I wouldn't know what to say, and what if she has a question?"

"Just tell her you want to show her a picture."

"You're the brains of this outfit, Jeffrey," Pablo said. "You're the master sleuth."

"Please, Jeffrey!" Marisol begged. "Do it for me and for Victor!"

Jeffrey sighed and picked up the phone. "I really hate to do this."

"Be very business-like," Marisol suggested. "Speak clearly and distinctly."

Jeffrey cleared his throat.

"Get right to the point," Pablo said. "Don't let her think you're calling for a date."

Marisol giggled and slapped Pablo on the arm.

"Thanks a lot!" Jeffrey said. He wiped his brow with his sleeve and dialed the number. "Maybe she won't be home."

The phone rang twice and Susie answered. "Hello?"

Jeffrey froze.

"Hello?" Susie repeated.

Jeffrey covered the mouthpiece and whispered to his friends. "It's her!"

They waved at him with their hands. "Talk to her!"

Jeffrey cleared his throat and spoke into the phone. "This is Jeffrey Jones."

Now it was Susie's turn to freeze. After an uncomfortable pause, she said, "What do you want?"

"I was wondering if you could do me a favor." Jeffrey grimaced. Pablo and Marisol giggled.

"A favor...? Me...?" Susie's voice turned suspicious. "What kind of favor?"

"I was wondering if I could show you a picture of a car, and if you could tell me if it's the same car you saw the other night by my house."

"You have a lot of nerve, Jeffrey Jones. After the way you treated me at the ice cream shop, and now you want me to do you a favor?"

"I'm sorry," Jeffrey mumbled.

"What?"

"I said I'm sorry!" Jeffrey's face flamed scarlet. Pablo and Marisol covered their mouths and bounced up and down on the couch as they fought to hold their laughter in.

"Hmmm. Well, I suppose I could give you five minutes. But only five minutes. And you better come over right now, because I'm leaving."

"I'll be right there!" Jeffrey slammed the phone down and slumped in his bean bag chair like a fighter who'd just gone twelve rounds. Pablo and Marisol wailed with laughter.

"Ha, ha, ha...!" Jeffrey yelled back at them. He grabbed the picture of Brittany James's car and stomped up the basement stairs.

Pablo and Marisol were still giggling as they walked with Jeffrey down the street to Susie's house. Jeffrey shushed them. "This is important business," he said.

Susie was waiting outside her front door, arms folded across her chest, tapping her foot impatiently on the porch, and wearing her silly felt hat.

"Hi, Susie," Marisol called as they approached.

"Hello," Susie said. Then to Jeffrey: "Mr. Jones, the great detective. Lemme see your picture."

Jeffrey offered her the photo. Susie snatched it out of his hand and studied it. She turned it sideways, then she turned it sideways the other way, then she turned it upside down. "Hmmm," was all she said.

"Well?" said Jeffrey. "Is it or isn't it?"

"It might be. But it was so dark that night, I really don't remember." She handed the picture back to Jeffrey. "Are you going to tell me what this case is all about or not?"

Jeffrey looked at Pablo, then at Marisol. "It's okay," Marisol said. "You can tell her."

Jeffrey told Susie the story of Victor's arrest and added, "We think the firecrackers were a warning to stop our investigation, and that's why we wanted to talk to you. Anyway, that's all we can tell you for now."

Susie stared back at them. "Wow, I'm sorry, Marisol. Maybe I can help you guys." Susie's mother called for her from inside the house. "I'll be there in a minute!" Susie yelled back. She turned to her classmates. "I have to go, you guys. But I want to help." She opened the front door and ducked inside her house.

"Come over later, Susie!" Marisol called after her. Jeffrey turned to her, horror-stricken. "What?" Marisol said. "Aren't four heads better than three?"

"Not when it's the head of Susie Norris," Jeffrey said. "I feel like Pandora and we just opened a box."

Pablo and Marisol laughed.

Chapter 23

Father Pat was an ancient priest, ordained before Vatican II, and he insisted on giving the traditional Latin Mass, with the traditional consecration of the host. At Father Pat's Mass, there was no music, no talking, and no Communion by hand, just pure adoration of God. He was assisted by traditional altar boys, and each Mass concluded with a prayer to St. Michael. Jeffrey loved it.

He sat in a pew by himself, tugging at his tie and waiting for the service to begin. The tie and the tight collar of his shirt made him uncomfortable, but he wore them out of respect for Father Pat and the original Catholic Mass. At Father Pat's Mass, women dressed modestly, with veils over their heads, and men wore jackets and ties, although in Jeffrey's mind, none of them looked or felt as out of place as he did.

His oddly-shaped body did not wear clothes well. The finest suit – the one that looked like a million dollars on a mannequin in a shop window – would appear dumpy and wrinkled the moment he put it on.

Jeffrey knew that God had compensated him for his physical shortcomings by giving him a brain, still it bothered him that he always looked sloppy and unkempt, no matter how much time he spent on his appearance. The heat in the church didn't help. It felt like a hundred degrees.

He turned to gaze over the crowd and the old wooden pew creaked under his weight. He saw Pablo entering with his parents and his eight-year-old sister, Maria, all dressed in their Sunday best. They looked like models. As they made their way up the center aisle, every fan stopped fanning and every eye turned their way.

Jeffrey's eyes swept right and were drawn to a girl his age in a white cotton dress. She was kneeling in a pew, with her eyes closed and her head bowed; a heavenly vision, with long dark eyelashes and a pair of delicate hands joined together in prayer. Her lips moved silently as she prayed, and though she wore a white veil over her hair, her face was visible. It was Marisol, and Jeffrey was knocked out by her beauty. He couldn't imagine a girl like that ever being attracted to someone like him and he felt suddenly depressed.

Another girl caught his eye. Her face was hidden by her veil, but the dress she wore fit her nicely and showed the beginnings of a shapely figure. Something about the girl was familiar, but Jeffrey couldn't quite put his finger on it. She turned to look behind her and Jeffrey saw that it was Susie.

Horrified, he snapped his head forward and faced straight ahead. Susie Norris! Was he insane? How could he have looked at her in that way? He could never forgive himself now. Quick, think of baseball player names, he told himself ... Anything to take his mind off what he had just done. Had she seen him looking at her? That would make it a hundred times worse! His face flamed red as he considered the possibility and he closed his eyes. I'm sorry, God, he prayed. Please forgive me! I'll never do that again!

Father Pat entered from the sacristy and Mass began.

Back at home, Jeffrey wanted to call Pablo, but the Reyes family always spent Sundays together. They were very strict about that. So Jeffrey spent the day reading, cleaning the house, and going over his notes on the case.

As the dark of night descended, his mind seemed to quicken. Something about Laura from the bowling alley kept coming back to him. He knew that she lied to them, but why? What was she hiding?

They had been operating on the assumption that Victor was innocent, but what if he wasn't? What if Victor was guilty and Laura was an accomplice to the crime? It was an unpleasant theory, but it made sense. It explained why Mr. Smithers had seen both Victor and Laura at the scene of the crime. And it explained why Laura had lied to them. With Victor in jail, she now had the painting all to herself. As long as Victor didn't talk, she would get away free. It would make her the essence of evil, he thought.

Of course, if Victor was guilty, Marisol and her mother would be heartbroken. So would Pablo. So would Father Pat. But truth was truth, and he had to pursue it.

He sat at his desk in the basement and asked himself over and over, just how Victor and Laura could have stolen the painting together, and where they could have hidden it. Could he prove they were guilty? Could he and Pablo trick Laura into revealing where the painting was hidden? He thought and he thought, and just when he felt like his brain was about to explode, the phone rang.

It was his parents, calling to check on him.

Everything is fine, he told them. We miss you, they said, and we'll be home soon.

He hung up and turned his thoughts back to the case. He was wondering if he should research Victor's arrest record when the phone rang again. His parents calling back..? They must have forgotten to tell him something. He reached for the phone. "Hello?"

It was the girl. "I told you to mind your own business."

"Who is this?"

"Violets are blue, roses are red, nosy people like you, wind up dead."

"Who is this?" Jeffrey demanded, his voice rising.

"We know where you live," she said, and the line clicked off.

Jeffrey hung up and stared at the phone, his blood racing. Now what?

A sharp knock came from the front door upstairs and Jeffrey's heart was in his throat. Somebody was outside!

He raced up the basement stairs and stood before the door. Another loud knock came from outside.

Jeffrey stopped breathing. "Who is it?" he yelled at the door.

The doorbell chimed.

"Who is it?!"

"It's me! Pablo!"

Relief flooded every cell of Jeffrey's body. He unlocked the door and swung it open. "Am I glad to see you," he said, as Pablo stepped inside.

"I told my dad your parents were out," Pablo explained, "and he said I could come over for a few minutes. But only on this one Sunday."

Jeffrey stuck his head out the front door and scanned the front yard and street. Satisfied, he swung the door shut and locked it securely.

"Man, you look white as a ghost," Pablo said.

Jeffrey told him about the phone call.

"The same girl as before?" Pablo asked.

"I think so. She said 'we' this time. '*We* know where you live.'"

Pablo whistled. "This is getting dangerous. We need to solve this mystery and fast." He strode into the living room, picked up the phone, and dialed a number.

Jeffrey followed him. "Who are you calling?"

Pablo held an index finger to his lips and spoke into the phone. "Hello, Mom? Can I spend the night at Jeffrey's house?" He put his hand over the mouthpiece and whispered to Jeffrey, "Are all the doors locked?"

Jeffrey nodded.

"Aw, come on, Mom. Jeffrey's all alone." He covered the mouthpiece with his hand again. "Should I tell her what happened?"

Jeffrey shook his head.

"Please, Mom! I'll be home first thing in the morning.... It's not that late.... Please ...! Alright ... Bye." Pablo's voice trailed off and he hung up. "She said to tell you she's sorry, but I should have asked her earlier. She wants me to come home right away."

"Go ahead," Jeffrey said, trying his best to sound brave. "I'll be okay."

"You sure?"

Jeffrey nodded.

Pablo gave his friend a pat on the back. "I'm sorry, man. I should have asked her earlier." He stepped to the front door and opened it. "Lock the door behind me."

Jeffrey bolted the door and watched out the window as Pablo got on his bike and rode off.

He was alone again, feeling small and vulnerable in the old house. He considered calling the police, but he knew they wouldn't take him seriously. What could they do about a prank call except take a report?

He thought about calling his parents, but there wasn't anything they could do. The news would only frighten them and ruin their trip.

Still, Jeffrey was not one to take chances. He turned the lights on all over the house, along with the television in the living room, hoping it might frighten away any potential intruders. It seemed to frighten the fish in the living room aquarium. They swam rapidly in circles with their eyes opened wide. Jeffrey figured they wouldn't mind a little excitement for one night.

Next, he went to the supply closet in the kitchen, where he kept all his sports equipment, and pulled out his Louisville Slugger baseball bat. He carried the bat downstairs to the basement and laid it close to his bed. He thought about getting his father's gun, and he would if he had to, but for now the bat would do. He told himself that if anyone tried to break into the house, he would swing first and ask questions later.

He went back to the supply closet, took a 25-foot long phone cord, and attached it to the landline in the living room. He strung the cord out and carried the phone down the basement steps. Stretched to its full length, the phone was now about five feet from his bed and would serve as a backup to his basement phone.

With the lights still burning and his clothes still on, he took his glasses off, set them on the nightstand table, laid down in bed, and stared up at the ceiling.

He said his prayers like that, lying in bed with his eyes open. Please, God, he prayed, please keep me safe. Please don't let anything happen to me.

He noticed his heart pounding faster than usual, much faster. He tried breathing slowly through his nose; long, slow, gentle breaths. It took a few minutes, but his heart slowed down.

His eyes were still open. He was afraid to close them, even with the lights on. He continued his slow breathing and soon his eyelids felt heavy, so heavy that it took an effort to hold them open. Maybe he'd close them for a moment, he thought. Nothing could happen in just a brief moment.

Soon he was drifting, drifting ... It was okay to sleep, he told himself. It was all okay. Only the house wouldn't let him.

Old houses have a language of their own, a language of creaks and groans. Jeffrey was used to it, and normally he had no trouble falling asleep, but tonight was different. Whenever he started to doze off, the house would crackle and moan and he would awaken with a start and reach for his baseball bat. Each time, he felt his heart leap to his throat. Each time, he reminded himself that it was just the old house.

As the night dragged on, he felt wearier and wearier, until not even the screaming house could keep him awake, and he fell asleep.

Chapter 24

Jeffrey awoke with a start before dawn. For a moment, he wondered why the lights were all on, and why he was still dressed in his clothes. Then he remembered. He put his glasses back on and his eyes darted around the basement. Nothing had happened, at least for one night.

He kneeled by his bedside and said his morning prayers. After a quick shower, he went out to water the front lawn.

The sun was starting to rise, with neighboring houses and trees forming silhouettes against its rays. The gray light of dawn revealed the back end of a garbage truck, rumbling down the street. Jeffrey frowned. He had forgotten to take out the trash the night before. His father was going to love that one.

An idea came to him: by pulling the weeds in his mother's garden, it might make up for his forgetting about the trash. He went to the garage, pulled on a pair of gardening gloves, and set to work.

An hour later he was almost done, when he heard someone shout his name. He looked up and saw Pablo, pedaling his bike as fast as his legs could turn. "Jeffrey, you okay?"

Pablo glided his bike into Jeffrey's driveway and hopped off, holding a bag in his hands.

Jeffrey smiled. "I didn't get much sleep, but I'm fine."

Pablo handed him the bag. "My mom felt bad about you being here all alone, so she made you some food: wild salmon and broccoli."

Jeffrey's eyes lit up. Moments later, they were ensconced in his kitchen. "Did you know that wild salmon is good for the brain?" Jeffrey said, just before taking a bite.

Pablo laughed. "That's why my mom made it for you. She said, 'If anyone can appreciate food for the brain, it's Jeffrey!' My dad said the same thing."

There was a sharp rap at the front door.

The boys looked at each other. Jeffrey thought of his baseball bat in the basement. Then they heard Marisol's voice. "Jeffrey, it's me!"

Pablo bounced out of his chair. "I'll get it," he said, running off.

"It has to be ocean-caught salmon," Jeffrey called, referring back to his fish, "like this. Not that farm-raised stuff." He took another bite and mused, "Man, this is good!"

Pablo returned to the kitchen with Marisol. She nodded at Jeffrey's plate. "That looks good. Did you make it yourself, Jeffrey?"

Chewing and smiling, Jeffrey shook his head.

"My mom made it," Pablo said. "She gave it to Jeffrey, because his parents are out."

"Oh, you should have told me, Jeffrey," said Marisol. "I'll tell my mom to make you some more food."

"You guys are too good to me," Jeffrey said. "Pablo, tell your mom thanks!"

Pablo told Marisol about the threatening phone call Jeffrey received and she gasped. "Do you think it's Laura?"

"We'll find out," Jeffrey said. "We're going to pay her a visit this morning."

An hour later, the boys were locking their bikes and walking towards the entrance of the bowling alley. "What are we going to say?" Pablo asked.

"We'll tell her we're thinking of going to visit Victor in jail," Jeffrey said. "And then we'll ask her if she wants to come with us. Technically, it won't be a lie, because I was going to ask Marisol's mom to drive us there. Watch her carefully, Pablo. Her reaction might give us a clue about why she lied to us and what she's hiding. We also need to get her last name so we can research her on the internet."

Pablo nodded. The heat wave that had gripped the city for the last few days had broken and the morning air felt significantly cooler. Pablo took it as a good sign as they crossed the parking lot. The doors of the bowling alley whooshed open automatically and they stepped inside.

The bowling alley was almost deserted. The only person in sight was the teenage girl behind the shoe rental counter. She looked like she hadn't moved since the last time the boys saw her. She was slouched over the counter in exactly the same way, staring wide-eyed at her phone, and chewing what may have been the exact same gum. Pablo wondered if she ever did any work at all.

The boys stepped up to the counter. Without looking up from her phone, the girl asked, "What size?"

"Size?" Jeffrey asked back.

"What size shoe you want?" The girl slid a finger across her phone.

"Actually, we're looking for Laura."

The girl blew a bubble of gum and popped it. "Laura doesn't work here anymore."

The boys exchanged a look. "What happened?" Jeffrey asked.

"Quit."

"When?"

"Last night."

"Do you know if she found another job?"

"Nope."

"Do you know where we can find her?"

"Nope. She quit without notice."

"Can you tell us Laura's last name?"

For the first time in their two visits, the girl lifted her eyes from her phone. They were cold eyes. "We don't give out personal information." She stared at the boys until they backed away from the counter.

"Wow. Now what?" Pablo asked quietly.

"I think it's a good sign," Jeffrey said. "It means we're close."

"You mean, like we scared her off?"

"Exactly. Remember the flak? Come on." He led Pablo to the nearest wall and began a slow circle of the bowling alley.

"Where are we going?" Pablo asked, following behind Jeffrey.

"You'll see."

They reached the refreshment area, where a row of plaques covered the wall. Each plaque cited an Employee of the Month and featured the winner's name and photo. "This is what I was looking for," Jeffrey said. "A lot of businesses give out awards like this."

They walked down the row of plaques and stopped at the month of March. Jeffrey pointed at it. "There she is."

Pablo studied the plaque. It showed a photo of Laura in a short-sleeved red work shirt, smiling behind the counter of the refreshment stand. Pablo read the inscription: "Laura Nichols."

Jeffrey wrote the name down. He and Pablo continued down the row of plaques and stopped at the month of May. It featured another photo of Laura in her red short-sleeved work shirt.

"There she is again," Pablo said. "Employee of the Month for March and again for May....That's twice in three months. She doesn't sound like someone who would quit a job without notice."

"Good observation," Jeffrey said, his eyes sparkling behind his glasses. "What else did you notice?"

Pablo could tell by Jeffrey's tone that his friend had just spotted another clue. He studied the plaque and Laura's photo. Then he went back to the plaque for the month of March. He did this several times, comparing them to each other. "The pictures are different," he told Jeffrey.

"And?"

Pablo looked at both photos again. "And Laura looks different."

"How?'

Pablo furrowed his brow. Jeffrey was testing him. He studied both photos again and then he saw it. "She has a tattoo in the second picture! On her arm, I can see it. It's not in the first picture."

Jeffrey smiled.

Pablo tapped at the photo with the tattoo. "Do you think she got that from Bob Sullivan?"

"That's impossible to say," Jeffrey replied. "But it's an idea worth pursuing. Those photos were probably taken a week or so after the month ended and she was declared the winner, so we'll say sometime between the first or second week of April, and the second week of June, which is now, she got that tattoo. It could be a fake one, too. You never know. Keep a lookout and tell me if you see anyone coming."

Jeffrey took out a pen and did a quick sketch of the tattoo, while Pablo kept watch.

"Did she have that tattoo when we first met her?" Pablo said. "I can't remember."

"Ah, it pays to be observant," Jeffrey said. "She was wearing a jacket when we met her, remember?"

"Oh, that's right. Now I remember. It was a jean jacket. She wore it over her red shirt."

"Good memory."

Jeffrey finished his sketch. The boys walked quickly towards the front door of the bowling alley. "Jeffrey, I think we're on to something. I can feel it," Pablo said.

"Keep thinking that way," Jeffrey said. "We'll solve this case yet." He gave Pablo a pat on the back and out they went.

The boys spent the afternoon at Pablo's house, helping his father clean the garage. When they finished, they helped Pablo's little sister, Maria, build a house for her pet turtle. A "turtle house" they called it. Jeffrey stayed for dinner and Mrs. Reyes was only too happy to slide him another heaping plate of wild salmon and vegetables.

She rested her chin on her hands and smiled at him from across the table. "When are your parents coming home, Jeffrey?"

"Two more days," Jeffrey replied between bites.

"Well, if you get hungry between now and then, you let me know."

"I will. Thank you, Mrs. Reyes."

"You're always welcome in this house, Jeffrey," Mr. Reyes said.

"Thank you, sir."

"I can make you a sandwich, too," said Maria.

The family laughed and Mr. Reyes reached over and tousled Maria's hair.

Chapter 25

It was early evening when the boys pedaled their bikes down Jeffrey's street. Marisol was waiting for them on Jeffrey's front porch, Susie beside her. They rose as the boys spun their bikes into Jeffrey's driveway. Marisol approached them. "How did it go with Laura?" she asked.

Jeffrey climbed off his bike and cast a wary eye at Susie. "Come on downstairs. We'll have a meeting and talk about it."

The boys walked their bikes to the garage. Marisol followed them. Susie waited on the porch.

"My mom went with Father Pat to visit Victor in jail today," Marisol said.

"How is he?" Pablo asked.

"Not good. He's scared and he kept telling them he didn't do it."

Jeffrey opened the garage door. The boys rolled their bikes inside.

"I wanted to go with them," Marisol continued, "but my mom wouldn't let me. She said I cried too much, and she can't take another broken heart."

Jeffrey nodded in Susie's direction. "What's she doing here?"

"I'm sorry, Jeffrey," Marisol said. "Susie said she had to come. She said you smiled at her in church."

"I didn't smile at her in church!" Jeffrey insisted, his voice rising.

"Shhh! She'll hear you!"

Jeffrey lowered his voice. "I didn't smile at her in church. If she said that, she's dreaming."

Marisol shrugged.

Jeffrey felt his face flushing and waved them all out of the garage.

Susie was aghast when they filed down the basement steps to Jeffrey's bedroom. She took one look at the hundreds of books scattered over every conceivable inch and shrieked, "What a mess!"

"It's just books, man," Jeffrey said.

Susie stepped gingerly around the piles of books covering the floor. "How does your mother stand it? Have you actually read all these things?"

"Most, not all," Jeffrey replied.

Susie eyed Jeffrey's unmade bed. "Don't tell me you actually sleep down here. Yuk."

"A man's home is his castle," Jeffrey said.

"This looks more like a barn."

Pablo and Marisol laughed and sat together on the sofa. Susie approached the beanbag chair. Jeffrey watched with horror. "Don't sit in that - "

It was too late. Susie plopped herself down on the chair and sank into it, her feet dangling off the floor and her eyes closed. "Ah, now this is a chair. So comfortable...." She opened her eyes and saw three faces staring back at her. "What?"

"That's Jeffrey's favorite chair," Pablo said.

"Well, excuse me!" Susie said, her words dripping with sarcasm. She climbed out of the chair and motioned to it with her arm. "Here, your highness, sit. I'm just a peasant in your castle."

"Relax and sit down," Jeffrey said.

"Sit down where?"

"Here!" Jeffrey shoved a teetering pile of books off a chair seat.

Susie gave him a mock salute and sat down.

Pablo laughed. "Jeffrey, tell Susie your theory on books!"

"What theory on books?" Susie asked.

Jeffrey sat in the beanbag chair. "Let's talk about the case."

"Wait, I want to hear Jeffrey's theory," Marisol said.

"Me, too," said Susie.

Jeffrey blushed. Pablo spoke for him: "Jeffrey doesn't like long books. His theory is that people who write long books are stuck-up and more in love with their words than in love with their readers. So except for the Bible, he refuses to read long books, no matter how good they are, because the writers are snobs."

Marisol laughed and clapped her hands. "I love it!"

Susie looked at Jeffrey askance. "Now I know you're insane."

Jeffrey blushed even redder.

Susie scanned the books covering the floor and scooped one up. "*Camouflage in Nature: The Indonesian Mimic Octopus*. Really, Jeffrey ..." She flipped through its pages. "Well, at least it's not a long book." She shook her head and tossed the book on his bed.

Jeffrey squirmed, but his words came out sharp. "The meeting will come to order." Everyone sat up straight. "Here are the facts we know so far ..."

Susie's cell phone rang. "Hold on," she said, and answered her phone. "Oh, hi, Gina.... What am I doing? Well, right now I'm in the messiest basement in America...."

Jeffrey stared at her in disbelief. Pablo and Marisol hid their smiles. Susie continued. "Yeah, *that* basement.... I don't know, I'll ask." Susie put her hand over the phone. "Guys, Gina wants to know if she can come over."

Jeffrey's withering look supplied the answer.

"Uh, actually, Gina, that's probably not a good idea. I'll call you when I get home." She clicked off, slid the phone back in her pocket, and smiled sweetly at Jeffrey.

"Continuing," Jeffrey said, "before we were so rudely interrupted ..."

Susie's phone rang again. Pablo and Marisol laughed out loud.

"Sorry! Sorry!" Susie said. She took out her phone and turned the ringer off. "There! I won't even answer it. How's that?" She put the phone back in her pocket and nodded at Jeffrey. "Continue, sir."

Jeffrey cleared his throat. "Here are the facts we know so far: Two Saturdays ago, Victor was cutting grass at Mr. Weeden's house, his regular Saturday job.

During that time, a valuable painting, worth half-a-million dollars, was stolen from inside the house. A witness across the street, Mr. Steven Smithers, says he saw Victor leaving the scene on his bicycle with the painting in his hands."

"But that part's not true," Marisol said.

Jeffrey glanced quickly at Marisol, and then at Pablo. "Mr. Smithers also says he saw a blond girl walking down Mr. Weeden's driveway about fifteen minutes later. The blond girl he saw looks similar to Victor's ex-girlfriend, Laura Nichols. They broke up about a week before the painting was stolen. This is Laura's picture."

He showed the photo of Laura to Susie. "She's guilty," Susie said.

"Of what?"

"Of everything. I can tell. Look at her face. That's a guilty face."

Jeffrey snatched the picture back and spoke to Pablo and Marisol. "You can see she's wearing a red shirt. She works at the bowling alley and that's her work uniform. The blond girl that Mr. Smithers saw was also wearing a red shirt. Is everyone with me so far?"

"Yes!" three voices said.

"Last Wednesday, Pablo and I went to Mr. Weeden's pawn shop and talked to both him and his assistant, Eddie. Mr. Weeden told us that Victor has a key to get into his garage, but not a key to the house where the painting was. He believes Victor used his key to get into the garage, and then picked the lock on the door that leads into the house, and stole the painting. And, because nothing else was stolen, Mr. Weeden believes, and Pablo and I agree, that the crime was not a random burglary, and that the painting was the target the thief was after."

Susie rubbed her hands together. "This is a good mystery."

Jeffrey sat up straighter. "After we talked with Mr. Weeden, Pablo and I went to a tattoo shop down the street owned by Bob Sullivan. He's the one who took the painting to the pawn shop to begin with. Pablo and I have concluded that he knew the painting was valuable and he took it to the pawn shop to hide it. We have also concluded that the painting was stolen before Bob Sullivan ever took it to the pawn shop."

"Okay, stop," Susie said. "How do you know all that?"

"We know Bob Sullivan is aware of the painting's value, because we had a conversation with him and he's an expert on art. And we know the painting is stolen, because there's no other reason for him to try and pawn a painting that's worth half-a-million bucks. Pablo discovered that he has a lot of celebrity clients, like Brittany James, who we saw entering his shop, so he shouldn't be desperate for money."

"Wait a second," Susie said. "You saw Brittany James? You mean, *the* Brittany James?"

"That's the one."

"You guys saw Brittany James? Oh, I can't stand her. That girl has more shoes than brain cells."

Pablo and Marisol laughed.

"I'm serious," Susie said. "She can't sing. She can't act. The only reason she's famous is because of her father. He's the one who got her into acting."

"Who's her father?" Jeffrey asked.

"Warren Stone."

"Warren Stone, the old actor?" Pablo asked.

"He's not that old."

"I didn't know he was her father," Marisol said.

"Nobody knows. She changed her name to hide it, and nobody that interviews her is allowed to mention it. She wants everyone to think she got famous on her own, when it was really all because of her family. A lot of actors are like that."

"The famous are rarely great, and the great are rarely famous," Jeffrey said.

Three bewildered faces turned to him.

"Think about it," Jeffrey said. "Anyway, we saw her going into the tattoo shop and arguing with Bob Sullivan, but we don't know what the argument was about. Later that night, someone threw a bunch of firecrackers at my house. Susie, you saw a car racing away."

"Right. I wish now I had paid more attention."

"I think the firecrackers were meant as a warning, to scare us off. And I suspect it came from either Mr. Weeden or Eddie, because they're the only ones we gave our business card to. Susie, I think the car you saw belongs to Brittany James. I think it's the same car that's in the photo we showed you."

"But why would she want to scare you?"

"We haven't solved that yet. All we know for sure is someone set out to steal the painting and they succeeded. Whoever the thief is, they had to know the painting was at Mr. Weeden's house. That leaves only four suspects that we know of: Victor, Eddie, Bob

Sullivan, and Mr. Weeden. Although, we don't know for sure if Bob Sullivan knew that Mr. Weeden moved the painting from the pawn shop to his house."

"Okay, stop again," Susie said. "How is Mr. Weeden a suspect? And why would he steal his own painting?"

"To collect the insurance money," Pablo said.

"Someone gave us some information on Mr. Weeden," Jeffrey said, "and Pablo researched it. Mr. Weeden twice collected insurance payments on buildings that he owned that were lost in questionable fires."

"What do you mean by questionable?" Susie asked.

"The fire investigators said it was arson, but they could never prove that Mr. Weeden did it. His handyman, a Vietnamese man who took the American name of Sam Britts, was arrested and released. Sam Britts claimed that Mr. Weeden set the fire himself and then tried to frame him for the crime. Two days after he was released from jail, Sam Britts was murdered."

"Ah, I think he did it," Susie said.

"You think who did what?" Jeffrey said.

"This Mr. Weeden, he stole his own painting."

"Why do you think that?"

"Just a hunch. He sounds guilty."

Jeffrey threw up his hands. "You can't keep saying people are guilty of this or that, because of the way they look or because of a hunch."

"Sure, I can. It's called women's intuition."

Pablo laughed out loud. Marisol elbowed him and he turned to her. "What?"

"Intuition doesn't count," Jeffrey said. "Neither do hunches, feelings, opinions, or lucky guesses. We need proof, we need facts."

"How about this," Susie suggested, "Mr. Weeden told Victor to move the painting to a different location and that's what your witness saw. So Victor did have the painting, but he wasn't stealing it. He was just following orders from his boss."

Marisol sat up and looked at Jeffrey with hopeful eyes.

Jeffrey shook his head. "Interesting theory, but Victor would have told the police that when they arrested him."

"Wait, I got it!" Susie cried. "Your witness, what's his name? Smithers? He and Mr. Weeden are in on it together! They hid the painting and Smithers is lying so he and Mr. Weeden can split the insurance money."

Jeffrey frowned.

"Come on, it's possible, isn't it?"

"It's possible, but it's highly unlikely. It's true that Mr. Smithers could be lying, but out of everyone involved in this case, he seems to be the most reliable one of all. At least, the most reliable one we've talked to. What do you think, Pablo?"

Pablo nodded. "I agree with Jeffrey. I don't think Mr. Smithers is lying." He glanced at Marisol and saw her staring back at him with hurt-filled eyes.

"Okay, how about this," Susie said. "Your witness, this Mr. Smithers, did see Victor, but not with the painting. Just something that looked like a painting. I mean, did he actually say he saw Victor with the stolen painting?"

Jeffrey consulted his notes. "He said he saw Victor with a painting."

"What if ...?" Susie began. "What if he saw Victor with a painting, but not *the* painting? What if Victor was carrying a different painting?"

Everyone looked at Jeffrey.

Jeffrey shrugged. "It's *possible*."

"That's it!" Marisol cried. "Victor is innocent!"

Susie squealed and clapped her hands. "Ha! Ha! I just solved your whole case!"

"Hold on," Jeffrey said. "You haven't solved anything. If Victor had another painting, why didn't he tell that to the police?"

"Does Victor know about the witness who saw him?" Pablo asked.

Jeffrey snapped his fingers. "That's a good point, Pablo." He turned to Marisol. "When the police arrested Victor, did they mention a witness?"

"I don't think so. I mean, I didn't see the whole thing. They just came in, arrested him, and searched the house. They didn't say much. They told me and my mom to stay out of their way."

"If Victor didn't know about the witness," Pablo began, "then maybe he didn't think about telling the police if he moved a painting. If Susie's right, then maybe Victor was just doing his job. Maybe Mr. Weeden told Victor to take a different painting to the pawn shop, while he arranged to hide the valuable one."

"You see," Susie said, "your witness is telling the truth. He did see Victor, but with a different painting."

"That makes sense to me," Marisol said, looking at Jeffrey and Pablo for approval.

"The question is," Susie wondered, "whether this Mr. Weeden is evil enough to steal his own painting and then frame Victor for the crime."

They were all quiet for a moment before Jeffrey spoke. "Greed is a powerful emotion, especially for someone who doesn't have a strong religious belief in right and wrong. We know Mr. Weeden is a cheapskate by some of the things he told us. Whether he's greedy enough to commit larceny and send an innocent man to jail is another question."

"Then you agree with my theory," Susie said.

"No, I don't," Jeffrey replied. "But we have to be open to all possibilities. I'm willing to discuss it."

They debated Susie's theory for the next two hours. Did Mr. Weeden steal his own painting and frame Victor? Was he really that evil? Were people in general naturally greedy and dishonest?

Jeffrey didn't say much. He mostly listened and observed.

When Susie checked the time on her phone, she popped out of her chair. "Oh, my gosh! It's late! I have to go!"

"Me, too," said Marisol.

"Me, three," said Pablo.

As they climbed the basement stairs, Susie said, "Marisol, you need a cell phone."

"My mom won't let me," Marisol replied.

"I'll talk to her," Susie said.

Pablo laughed. "I'm sure that'll go over big."

"I'll talk to your mom, too," Susie said and they all laughed.

The girls said goodnight and went out the front door. Pablo lingered behind, and he and Jeffrey went into the living room. They heard the voices of Marisol and Susie from outside as they walked off, and then the voices faded out, and all was quiet and dark, save for the bubbling water of the aquarium and an eerie glow from the aquarium lights.

"We can talk a little more freely now without the girls," Jeffrey said. "I hate to say this, or even think it, but we have to consider Victor a strong suspect."

Pablo froze. "You don't think Mr. Weeden tried to frame Victor, like Susie suggested?"

Jeffrey shook his head. "When you consider all the facts, it doesn't make logical sense. And one more thing, a thief almost always criticizes the person they're stealing from. They exaggerate the other person's faults, make up lies, you name it, in order to justify their crime.

Mr. Weeden didn't do that. He didn't say anything bad about Victor at all. If he was out to frame Victor, he would have told us what a lousy worker Victor was, how he couldn't trust him, and all that."

"Like the way Laura talked about Victor," Pablo said.

"Exactly. The way Laura talked about Victor tells me she's guilty of something. I just don't know what."

"What if Mr. Weeden knows all that and he deliberately talked good about Victor in order to fool us and not look guilty?"

Jeffrey laughed. "If Mr. Weeden did that, then he's a genius and smarter than both of us, which I doubt. Now I've been over this case backwards and forwards. I know Bob Sullivan is hiding something, and I know Laura is lying and she's somehow mixed up in all this. Maybe she's an accomplice. Until we talk to Mr. Smithers again and ask him specifically about the painting he saw Victor carrying, I'm not buying Susie's theory. Although I do give her credit for being creative. To me, there's just no way of getting around Mr. Smithers's testimony. He saw Victor leaving the scene with a painting, he reported it to the police, and they made an arrest. If we can't solve that, then we have no case. And if we have no case, then we're not going to be able to get Victor out of jail."

Pablo nodded grimly and stared at the floor. "So what do we do?"

"I'm going to stay up late and do some research on my mom's computer. Keep thinking about the case. We're smart enough to solve this mystery, I know we are." He gave Pablo a pat on the shoulder and clattered down the basement stairs to his room.

Pablo stood in front of the aquarium and stared at the fish. He knew Jeffrey was smart and probably right about everything. Odds were they'd never be able to help Marisol by getting Victor out of jail.

Crickets chirped as Pablo walked his bicycle slowly down Jeffrey's driveway. He saw Marisol standing on her front porch, bathed in a beam of moonlight, waiting for him. She watched him with gentle eyes as he walked over to her. "What did you and Jeffrey talk about?" she said.

"We talked about the case."

"Does he believe Susie's idea?"

Pablo thought about lying, but he couldn't. He looked at Marisol and shook his head. "No, Jeffrey doesn't buy it. But he thinks we can still solve the case."

Marisol lowered her head and twisted her hands, one over the other. "Thank you, Pablo," she said quietly.

"For what?"

"For being my friend. For helping me. I know you and Jeffrey are going to get Victor out of jail, I just know it."

She looked up into his eyes and smiled softly. Then she opened the door and went inside. Pablo stood alone in the dark.

Chapter 26

It was impossible for Pablo to sleep. Something on the back of his mind nagged him. What was it? He tossed and turned, unable to shake a strange sense of unfinished business. Every time he started to doze off, his mind would rebel and snap his body back to attention. He felt as if the solution to the entire mystery was right in front of him, yet he couldn't quite grasp it.

As dawn neared, he couldn't take it anymore. He threw off his covers and swung his feet out of bed. Sitting on the side of his bed, his head hurt and his stomach growled. Might as well go to the kitchen and get something to eat.

He crept quietly out of his room, so as not to wake anyone. The hall was dark, but a light was on in the kitchen. Maybe someone forgot to turn it off. He was shocked to find his father, dressed for work and eating his breakfast at the kitchen table. His father was just as shocked to see him.

"Pablo! What are you doing up so early?"

"I couldn't sleep," Pablo said. He slid into a chair, across the table from his father.

Mr. Reyes gazed at him with concern. "What's wrong?"

Pablo shook his head. "Nothing. It's just that me and Jeffrey are working on a mystery and it's a tough one. What are you doing up so early?"

Mr. Reyes frowned deeply. "It's tough at work now, son. A lot of layoffs. A lot of people losing their jobs. So I'm unleashing my secret weapon."

Pablo perked up. "Your secret weapon?"

"I never told you my secret weapon? Well, it's time you learned." Mr. Reyes held up his thumb. "Show up early." He raised his index finger to join his thumb. "Stay late." His middle finger joined the other two. "Smile all the time."

Pablo laughed. "How is that a secret weapon?"

"I'll explain it like this," his father said. "Suppose you're the boss. You have ten people working for you. One person doesn't show up, because he's sick, or just pretending to be sick. Two people are late. Six are on time. But one employee is there fifteen minutes early, already setting up and getting ready for the day. Who looks best in your eyes?"

"The one who got there early."

His father nodded. "Now you got nine people at work, because one never showed up, remember? One of those nine gets sick in the middle of the day, or has some kind of emergency, and has to leave. Seven workers are counting the seconds till the clock strikes closing time, and when it does, they're out the door like a shot. But one worker stays late. He tidies up and double-checks everything. He asks the boss if there's anything else he can do. If the boss says no, then and only then, does he go home. Who looks best?"

"The one who stays late."

Mr. Reyes nodded again. "Okay, now of those ten workers, one is never there. She's sick, she's late, she always has some kind of drama going on. Another is mad at the world. He hates the job, hates the customers, he hates everything. Nobody wants to be around him. Three others aren't bad, but they don't do anything special, either. They're wishers. One wishes she had a boyfriend, another wishes he had a girlfriend, and the third wishes he had any friend at all."

Pablo laughed.

Mr. Reyes continued. "Now we have five workers left. Four are okay. They say 'please' and 'thank you', but they never do anything to stand out. Now our last worker, he's the one who comes in early and leaves late. And while he's at work, he has a smile all the time. He makes everyone feel good, he does his job well, and he always, always does more work than he's paid for. Who's your favorite?"

"The last one," Pablo said. "The smiling one."

"There you go. That's my secret weapon. Show up early, stay late, and smile all the time."

"Does it work?"

"You're the boss, you tell me."

Pablo smiled. "I get it."

"You do that, son, and you'll always have a job. You do that, and you mix in a little brains, and a little ambition, and there's no telling how far you'll go. That's what my father taught me, and now I've taught it to you." He checked his watch. "Look at the time. I have to run if I want to get to work early."

He hopped out of his chair and rinsed his plate in the sink.

"I'm doing your secret weapon now, Dad," said Pablo. "I'm up early to work on our mystery."

"Good for you, Pablo. You got the idea." He wiped his hands on a towel and gave Pablo a pat on the back. "I'll see you tonight."

"Bye, Dad."

Mr. Reyes went out the door, leaving Pablo alone at the kitchen table. Pablo thought about his father's "secret weapon" and smiled. He wondered if other fathers passed on advice to their sons like that. He supposed that they must. They were probably that way with their daughters, too, he thought. Kind of like what Susie said about Warren Stone and the way he helped his daughter, Brittany James, get into acting and become famous. It didn't seem to help her much, because she was always in trouble, but at least her father had tried. At least he'd ...

A thought flashed into Pablo's mind and he sat straight upright in his chair. Of course! That was it! The key to the whole case! Why hadn't he thought of it before?

He picked up the phone, but the sun wasn't even up yet. Jeffrey would still be asleep. Besides, Pablo still had to research his idea. He hung up the phone and ran down the hall.

A quick shower and he threw on his clothes and raced back down the hallway. His mother stepped out of her bedroom and he passed her like a blur.

"Pablo, where are you going?" she asked, still sleepy and pulling her robe tight around her.

"To get an innocent man out of jail!" Pablo shouted, and he bolted out the door without even stopping for breakfast.

Pablo was first in line when the library opened. Using the computer, he researched Brittany James and her father, Warren Stone. It took two hours, but he found what he was looking for and printed the pages with trembling hands. By noon, he was at Jeffrey's house, knocking loudly on the door.

When Jeffrey didn't answer, Pablo knocked again and rang the doorbell. He heard muffled footsteps approaching from inside the house. The door swung open and Jeffrey stood before him, dressed in jeans and a wrinkled T-shirt, looking like he'd been up all night.

"I'm glad you're here, Pablo," Jeffrey said, as he moved aside to let his friend in. "I've got some stuff to show you."

"I've got some stuff to show you," Pablo said, a sheaf of papers in his hand.

"You go first," said Jeffrey.

They went down to the basement and Pablo began. "We thought there were only four people who could have known that Mr. Weeden had the painting at house: Victor, Eddie, Bob Sullivan, and Mr. Weeden. But there's a fifth person who also knew: Brittany James."

Jeffrey's eyes widened.

Pablo continued. "I did some research at the library. Like Susie said, Brittany James got into acting through her father, Warren Stone. He was a big movie star in the eighties and nineties. Five years ago, when Brittany first became famous, she began having problems with drugs and alcohol. A feud broke out between Brittany and her father, and they stopped talking to each other. I had to search all over the internet, but I found this picture of Warren Stone and Brittany at his house in the Hollywood Hills, just before she became famous."

He showed Jeffrey one of the pages he printed at the library. It featured a picture of Warren Stone, seated on a sofa with his daughter, Brittany. Behind them on the wall hung the painting "Flowers of Spain."

"That's our painting!" Jeffrey shouted.

"That picture is five years old. If Warren Stone owned the painting five years ago, then he probably owns it today. I believe that Brittany James stole the painting from his house and then took it to Bob Sullivan to ransom back to her father."

"Your deduction is excellent!" Jeffrey said.

"I also think that when Warren Stone discovered the painting was stolen, he suspected his daughter, but he didn't go to the police, because he didn't want her to get arrested. I think he confronted her about it. At that point, Brittany and Bob Sullivan got scared and hid the painting at the pawn shop, in case anyone came looking for it."

"I think you're right," Jeffrey said. "Your logic has convinced me."

"The only problem with my theory is it still doesn't help Victor, or prove that he didn't steal the painting."

Jeffrey pointed at the other papers in Pablo's hand. "What are those?"

"More information on Warren Stone." Pablo handed the papers to Jeffrey. "He's appearing at a luncheon today in Beverly Hills. Then later tonight he's flying to Europe to start work on another movie."

Jeffrey sat on the side of his bed and studied the papers. He stopped at a picture of Warren Stone dressed in a costume with long blue hair, and tapped it with his finger. "What's this?"

"That's from a super hero movie," Pablo explained.

"What's with the hair?"

"Must be a wig. Nobody has hair like that."

Jeffrey sat silently on his bed for a long moment, thinking hard. Then he spoke quietly. "Pablo, you've solved the whole case."

Pablo looked stunned. "I have?"

Jeffrey reached on his nightstand and grabbed some papers he had printed from his mother's computer. "Look at these." He showed Pablo some images of tattoos. "Those are from Bob Sullivan's website. Look familiar?"

Pablo studied the images. "They look like Laura's tattoo, the one we saw in that picture of her at the bowling alley."

"It's the exact same tattoo," Jeffrey said. He showed Pablo the sketch he made of Laura's tattoo when they were at the bowling alley and compared it to the images he printed out. "See? It's a Japanese kanji tattoo, which according to his website, is Bob Sullivan's specialty."

"So Laura got her tattoo from Bob Sullivan?"

"That's the likely deduction. Look at this." He showed Pablo another picture he printed out. "I found it on the internet."

Pablo looked at the picture. "It's Laura and Eddie!" he cried. "They know each other!"

"Eddie's last name is Williams," Jeffrey said. "I ran a background check on him and found out he's been arrested nine times. His network page has tons of pictures of him and Laura. It's a setup! The whole thing is a setup! And your discovery ties the whole case together."

Jeffrey grabbed his notes and showed Pablo what he wrote after they left the pawn shop: Triple O Hardware, Mel's Costume and Wig Shop, Phil's Liquor, Tattoo Shop. "Come on," he said.

They ran upstairs to his mother's computer. Jeffrey looked up the website to Mel's Costume and Wig Shop, found the phone number, and called it. He held the phone so Pablo could listen to the call. A teenage girl answered.

Jeffrey took a deep breath and spoke in an older, huskier voice. "Hi, I bought a wig there a week or two ago. Do you remember me?"

"Is this the guy from the pawn shop?" the girl asked.

"Yeah, that's me. Do you remember my name?"

"It's Eddie, right? How was your costume party?"

"It was great, thanks. Um, my boss is coming, I have to go. Bye." He hung up and he and Pablo faced each other.

"Eddie?" Pablo said.

"Of course, don't you see? With a long-haired wig and his bicycle, he could look just like Victor, and that's who Mr. Smithers saw. Laura goes in first, to distract Victor. She lies and tells him she wants to get back together. Then while they're talking or making out or whatever in the back yard, Eddie slips in and steals the painting. He wears a wig just in case anyone sees him, like Mr. Smithers. After Eddie's gone, he calls her and tells her he's in the clear. Then she leaves. That's why Mr. Smithers saw her walking down the driveway ten minutes later."

"But how did Eddie get into Mr. Weeden's house?"

"Remember when Mr. Weeden took his nap? He put his keys in his jacket pocket, and then draped his jacket over a chair. Humans are creatures of habit. He probably does that every day, and Eddie knows it. All he has to do is sneak in there quietly while Mr. Weeden is sleeping, slide the keys out of his jacket pocket, and then run next door to the hardware store and make a copy. Then he returns and slips the keys back into Mr. Weeden's pocket before he wakes up."

"That's how Eddie got that new tattoo he had on his arm when we saw him," Pablo said. "Mr. Weeden told us he doesn't pay Eddie very much money, but if Eddie helped Bob Sullivan by stealing the painting ..."

"Exactly," Jeffrey said. "It's part of his payoff. Plus a stake in the ransom money, I'm sure."

"Is that how Laura got her tattoo, also?"

"Yep, they're all in on it. And they have Warren Stone in a trap. If he calls the police, his daughter gets another arrest and goes to jail. If he doesn't pay the ransom, then Bob Sullivan or Eddie, or someone else can go to the police and pretend to be heroes who recovered a stolen painting. Brittany still goes to jail. Mr. Stone has to pay the ransom, and if he's leaving for Europe tonight, then the payoff must be today, probably someplace in public, probably that luncheon today in Beverly Hills."

Pablo checked his watch. "That luncheon starts in exactly thirty minutes."

"Then we have no time to waste. Come on!"

They grabbed their papers and ran next door to Marisol's house. Mrs. Rodriguez opened the door and the boys both started talking at once.

"One at a time! One at a time!" she shouted.

"Mrs. Rodriguez, we have to talk to you," Jeffrey said. "It's an emergency. It's about Victor!"

She led them to the kitchen, the boys chattering the whole time. Marisol was in her room with Susie. They heard the commotion and came running.

Jeffrey and Pablo showed them their papers and told them everything they'd discovered. Mrs. Rodriguez and the girls listened in stunned silence. "Did the detective who arrested Victor leave you his contact information?" Jeffrey asked Mrs. Rodriguez.

"He left me his card. He said if we found the painting to call him."

"Call him immediately," Jeffrey said. "Tell him everything we've told you, and tell him to meet us at the luncheon where we think he'll find the stolen painting. Come on, Pablo!"

"Wait!" cried Mrs. Rodriguez. "You boys can't go there! It's too dangerous!"

"The police don't know what Bob Sullivan looks like, or Eddie, or Laura. Pablo and I can show them!" He and Pablo dashed out of the kitchen and out the front door.

"Wait for me!" Marisol cried, and ran after them.

"And me!" cried Susie.

"Marisol! Girls!" Shrieked Mrs. Rodriguez. She ran to the front door and saw them all racing down the street.

"Come back!" she yelled, but no one heard her.

She slammed the door and began a frantic search for the police detective's card.

Chapter 27

Shoes slapped against pavement. Four runners huffed and puffed. Pablo led the way, striding long and easy, Marisol behind him, then Susie, and Jeffrey last. The subway ride from North Hollywood to Los Angeles had taken twenty minutes, followed by another twenty minutes on a bus to Beverly Hills, and now this mad dash down Wilshire Boulevard to the hotel, which loomed before them.

"Wait up!" Jeffrey called. He stopped and bent at the waist, hands on his knees, gasping for air.

The others slowed and came back to him.

"Come on, inspector," said Pablo, the only one of them not winded.

Susie was huffing and puffing herself, but she wagged a finger at Jeffrey. "I told you to lose weight back at the ice cream shop."

Jeffrey wanted to tell her off, but he hadn't the strength. He kept his head down, sucking in huge gulps of air. He took off his glasses and wiped the sweat from his face.

"Jeffrey, pretend you're a superhero," Marisol said, "and you're chasing villains, which you are."

Jeffrey laughed in spite of himself and straightened up. His ribs ached and his legs felt like rubber, but he put his glasses back on and nodded at Pablo. The race resumed.

The luncheon was ending as they arrived. Under a large canopy, and by the shimmering blue water of the pool, were tables, chairs, and a podium for speakers. A sea of smartly-dressed movie people milled about, greeting each other with a show of smiles and hugs. Small talk and quiet laugher buzzed the air. Silverware and plates clinked against each other as waiters in white jackets began to clean up. Jeffrey surveyed the situation. He had his second wind now and he led the way, slipping past bodies in the crowd. The others followed.

"Jeffrey, over there!" Pablo pointed across the crowd to Bob Sullivan, wearing a suit and standing by the pool. "And looks who's with him." Standing close by were Eddie, wearing a dress shirt and tie, and holding a cylinder in his hands, and Laura, dressed in a long gown. Pablo turned to the girls. "It's the guy who owns the tattoo shop, and Eddie and Laura."

Marisol nodded. "I recognize Laura."

"It looks like Eddie's holding a pipe," Pablo said.

"It's hollow," said Jeffrey. "Canvas paintings can be cut out of their frames and rolled up without damaging them. He probably has the painting inside. Susie, call the police. Tell them there's an art-napping in progress."

"Art-napping?"

Before Jeffrey could respond, Pablo grabbed his arm and pointed again. "Warren Stone!"

Jeffrey looked where Pablo was pointing. A handsome man in his late-forties walked slowly through the crowd, heading towards the pool and carrying a small leather satchel.

"That's him, all right," Jeffrey said. "And he's got the ransom money in that case he's carrying." He turned to the girls. "Susie, give the police descriptions of the two men by the pool and the blond girl. Come on, Pablo!" He raced ahead, dodging his way through the crowd, Pablo and Marisol right behind him.

"Wait!" cried Susie. She trailed behind, frantically punching numbers on her phone.

Laura saw them first, heading their way through the crowd. She nudged Eddie and nodded in their direction. Eddie looked and his face hardened like stone. He tightened his grip on the pipe.

Warren Stone neared the pool and nodded grimly at Bob Sullivan. Jeffrey saw them and pushed his way wildly through the crowd. As the actor held the satchel out to Bob Sullivan, Jeffrey shouted, "Mr. Stone, don't pay the ransom!"

His shout silenced the murmur of small talk that hung over the pavilion. Heads turned. Warren Stone froze. Bob Sullivan saw Jeffrey and Pablo emerge from the crowd and a wave of recognition rippled over his face. He opened his mouth to speak, but Jeffrey beat him to it: "I'm making a citizen's arrest!" Jeffrey grabbed a waiter by the arm and pointed at Bob Sullivan, Eddie, and Laura. "Arrest those three, they're all thieves!"

Anger flashed in Eddie's eyes. He lunged at Pablo and swung the pipe at his head. Pablo ducked and dove forward, grabbing Eddie by the closet ankle. In one smooth move, Pablo pulled up on the ankle and drove his shoulder into Eddie's waist. Eddie teetered on one leg, arms flailing, and toppled backwards. His head hit the hard floor with a thud.

Women screamed. Men, known for playing tough action heroes on the screen, ran for the nearest exit.

Pablo snatched the pipe from Eddie and threw it back to Marisol. Bob Sullivan grabbed for Mr. Stone's satchel, but the actor wouldn't let go. The two men struggled, grabbed each other by the throat, and fell into the pool. More women screamed. The crowd surged back.

Eddie got his feet under him and threw a wild punch at Pablo, grazing his cheek. Jeffrey charged forward and barreled into Eddie with all his weight. The two of them hit the pool, sending up a tremendous splash. Pablo jumped in after them and wrapped an arm around Eddie's neck. Marisol screamed.

An army of waiters and security personnel descended on the scene. Marisol grabbed at them and pointed wildly. "Arrest him! And him! And her!" As Marisol pointed, Laura lifted the ends of her long dress and fled through the crowd. Waiters and security guards plunged into the pool. Susie spoke frantically into her phone, giving directions to the police dispatcher. Sirens wailed in the distance.

Amid all the commotion, Brittany James, with the collar of her jacket turned up, and her face hidden behind dark glasses and a floppy hat, walked briskly through the crowd. She strode out the front door of the hotel as Mrs. Rodriguez, accompanied by a police detective and several uniformed officers, rushed in.

Mrs. Rodriguez and the detective arrived at the pool to see a dozen men dragging Eddie and Bob Sullivan out of the water and handcuffing them. Warren Stone was also handcuffed until his voice boomed, "Do you know who I am?" As a policeman unlocked his cuffs, Mr. Stone said, "What about the blond girl that was here?"

"We caught her outside," the policeman said. The actor only grunted.

Jeffrey and Pablo sat soaked by the side of the pool. Marisol sat at Pablo's side, her fingers tracing a welt on his cheek. At Jeffrey's urging, the police detective opened the pipe and found the priceless painting. "What about Victor?" Mrs. Rodriguez asked the detective.

"If your story pans out, and it looks like it will, we'll be releasing him soon. Thank these young detectives." He motioned at Jeffrey and Pablo, and walked away. Mrs. Rodriguez started to cry.

Jeffrey pulled a soggy business card from his pocket and handed it to Pablo. "I had these printed up in advance, and now you've earned it. Congratulations."

Pablo looked at the card. It read:

Pablo smiled.

Marisol hugged him and kissed his cheek. "I'm so proud of you," she gushed. "And you, Jeffrey!"

"Thanks," Jeffrey replied, "but there's still one more mystery left to solve."

"What's that?" Marisol asked.

Jeffrey looked her straight in the eye. "The murder of Sam Britts."

Chapter 28

For Pablo, they were back where they began with the mailman burglar. Jeffrey was set to outsmart another criminal, only this time the crime was murder.

The boys sat in the back seat of Mr. Kozlowski's car, across the street from Mr. Weeden's pawn shop. Jeffrey had removed his glasses, slicked back his hair, and dressed in a suit and tie. To anyone but Pablo, he was completely unrecognizable. On his lap was a trumpet case.

Mr. Kozlowski's friend, Ben Hodges, a retired police officer, sat in the passenger seat, watching the pawn shop windows with a pair of binoculars. "Weeden's gone in the back," he announced tersely. He lowered the binoculars, turned to the back seat, and nodded at Jeffrey. "Okay, son. Let's see if you're right."

The boys looked at each other. Pablo's heart was beating so fast, he thought it would explode. The four of them piled out of the car, crossed the street, and slipped quietly inside the pawn shop. Pablo and the two men hid themselves behind a display. Jeffrey stepped up to the counter, the trumpet case under his arm, and called out cheerily in a high-pitched English accent, "Hello? Is anybody home?"

Mr. Weeden's voice carried from the back, "Hold on, I'm coming!" Seconds later, he shuffled into Jeffrey's view.

"Hello!" Jeffrey greeted him. "I have an instrument for you to inspect." He placed the trumpet case on the counter.

Mr. Weeden took one look at Jeffrey and spoke harshly, "You have to be eighteen to be in this shop!"

"I'm terribly sorry," Jeffrey responded. "I didn't know. You see, I'm on holiday from Britain."

"I don't give a rip where you're from. I don't do business with kids. So take your instrument and shove off."

"Certainly, sir. I understand. But if you won't do business with me, won't you please just look at it and tell me its worth?" Jeffrey popped the latches on the case and lifted its lid. "Please, sir?"

"Alright," Mr. Weeden grumbled, "but be quick about it." He stepped behind the counter.

Jeffrey reached into the case and removed the trumpet he found in Mr. Kozlowski's garage. He handed it over.

As Mr. Weeden took the instrument in his hands, a look of veiled recognition swept over his face.

"It's a perfectly fine instrument, you see?" Jeffrey said. "Except for one minor flaw. It has some tiny red specks just inside the bell." Jeffrey pointed. "It's blood, I suppose, but they're really very tiny specks. I suspect they could be cleaned off. Odd place for blood, don't you think?"

Mr. Weeden glanced at the trumpet's bell and his hands began to tremble. "Where did you get this?" he asked quietly.

"Oh, I picked it up at one of your American flea markets, but I no longer want it. They won't take it back, so I thought I'd try you."

"I'll give you ten dollars for it," said Mr. Weeden, and he turned to his cash register.

"Ten dollars? Surely, you must be joking."

"This is a piece of junk. I'll give you fifteen."

"No."

"Well, how much do you want?"

"I thought you were a reputable businessman, but I can see that you're not. I'll take my trumpet back please." Jeffrey reached out his hand, but Mr. Weeden pulled back and held the trumpet tight against his chest.

"Look, kid, if you paid more than ten bucks for this thing, you were ripped off. I'll give you fifty dollars for it." He rang open the cash register and pulled out a pair of twenties and a ten. "Here, take it," he said, offering the money to Jeffrey.

"No, thank you. Please return my instrument."

"How much do you want?" Mr. Weeden practically screamed. "This is junk and I'm offering you fifty dollars!"

"You can keep your fifty dollars. I'll take my trumpet please." Jeffrey reached over the counter for the instrument, but Mr. Weeden pulled back sharply. "What are you doing?" Jeffrey shrieked. "That's my property!"

"I'll give you a hundred dollars for it!"

"Absolutely not!"

"Two hundred!"

"No!"

"Five hundred!"

"No, no, no!" Jeffrey reached for the trumpet. Mr. Weeden slapped his hand away. Jeffrey stared at him, wild-eyed. "Why, it's the blood, isn't it? That's why you want the trumpet so bad!"

Mr. Weeden stared back. "Who put you up to this?"

"Up to what?"

"Who told you to bring this trumpet in here?"

"It was a ghost, actually."

"A what?"

"A ghost. A ghost by the name of Sam Britts."

Mr. Weeden froze. A dark cloud descended over his face.

"You killed him, didn't you?" Jeffrey said. "Bashed his head in with that trumpet you're holding, because he knew you set fire to your own building. That's his blood still on the murder weapon, isn't it? I think the police would be very interested in seeing that trumpet."

Mr. Weeden lowered his head and glowered at Jeffrey under his heavy eyebrows. Without a word, he went to the front door and locked it.

Jeffrey tensed and took a step back. Mr. Weeden turned to him, his breathing slow and deliberate, sweat glistening on his forehead. He stared at Jeffrey and rolled up his sleeves. "You're a smart kid, aren't you? Think you can come in here and blackmail me?"

He stepped behind the counter and pulled out the leather blackjack. Slapping the blackjack against his palm, he advanced slowly on Jeffrey, his eyes glaring with menace. "Yes, I killed him. Sam Britts saw something he shouldn't have, so I bashed his head in with that trumpet, just like you said. I killed him, and now I'm going to kill you."

"No, you're not," said Ben Hodges, holding a gun in his hand and stepping into view with Mr. Kozlowski and Pablo behind him. "You're going to jail."

Chapter 29

"Somebody's having a party," Jeffrey's father observed as he steered the family car into the driveway.

Jeffrey smiled from the backseat as he looked out the window and saw a crowd of happy people gathered amid picnic tables and folding chairs in Marisol's front yard. Children played and chased balloons, dogs barked, and mariachis sang and played their guitars.

"Is it somebody's birthday?" asked Jeffrey's mother.

"I don't think so," Mr. Jones mused. "Maybe they just decided to throw a party." He parked the car and they all got out.

"They're celebrating Victor's release from jail," Jeffrey said, as if it were nothing. He hadn't told his parents anything about the events of the last few days. He knew they'd be angry. He knew they wouldn't understand.

Jeffrey's mother turned to him with a look of horror. "Jail? Victor was in jail?"

"He was falsely arrested," Jeffrey said, as he and his father pulled heavy travel bags from the car. "He's free now. He didn't do anything."

"Well, that's good news," his mother said. She unlocked the front door and held it open. Jeffrey and his father entered the house and hauled their bags down the hallway. Music and laughter from the party was muted, but still audible inside the house.

"How were you, son?" his father asked.

"Fine."

"Any trouble? Any problems?"

"No, not really."

They entered the master bedroom and dropped their bags. Mr. Jones gave Jeffrey a pat on the back. "Your mother and I are taking you out to dinner tonight."

Jeffrey blinked behind his glasses. "Thanks, but can we go tomorrow?"

"Why tomorrow?"

"I want to go to the party next door."

Mrs. Jones entered and opened the heavy drapes that covered the windows. Late afternoon sunlight flooded the room. "Did you tell Jeffrey to get ready for dinner?"

"He wants to go tomorrow."

"Tomorrow? Why tomorrow?"

"He wants to go to the party outside."

"You don't want to have dinner with us, Jeffrey?" his mother asked. "We haven't seen you since Saturday."

"Yeah, I want to, Mom. But Pablo's next door, and some of my other friends, and can I go over there?"

His parents exchanged a look.

"Go say hi to your friends," his father said, "and then come back."

"I can't stay at the party?"

"We've been gone all this time," his mother said, "and now you don't want to have dinner with us? We were hoping you'd be excited. We want to give you a reward for watching the house and taking care of everything."

Jeffrey looked from one parent to the next.

"Do what your father suggested," his mother said, her voice softer. "Say hi to your friends and come back. We'll wait for you."

Jeffrey hung his head and walked out.

"Strange boy," said his father.

"Very strange," said his mother.

The phone rang in the living room.

"I'll get it," Mr. Jones said, and walked out of the room.

Jeffrey sulked down the hall. For three glorious days he'd been his own boss, and now, here he was, just a kid again and following orders. He opened the front door and stepped outside. The party had doubled in size. The music was louder. The shrieks of the children were wilder. Jeffrey started across the yard.

Father Pat was the first to see him. He hurried over and shook Jeffrey's hand. "Congratulations, Jeffrey! I knew you could do it!"

"Thank you, Father."

Father Pat put his arm around Jeffrey and called to the others, "Jeffrey's here!"

Smiling faces rushed in from all directions. Pablo led the pack. With a wide grin on his face, he shook Jeffrey's hand, followed by others, many others. Marisol tried to reach Jeffrey, but she was squeezed out by Mrs. Rodriguez, who, to the laughter of everyone, threw her arms around Jeffrey and kissed his cheek.

Victor approached with a humble, but happy glow, and shook hands with both Jeffrey and Pablo. "Man, you guys are the best," he said. "You saved my life." The crowd around them cheered and applauded.

Mr. Smithers, with his toothy grin, appeared in front of Jeffrey. "Now you must tell me how you solved this case!"

"Yes! Yes! We want to hear!" voices called out.

"Let Pablo tell it," Jeffrey said. "He can explain it better than me."

Mr. Smithers and the crowd turned to Pablo, pressing in and flooding him with questions. Jeffrey slipped quietly away. As he started back across the yard, he heard his name and turned to see Marisol running towards him, with Susie close behind.

Marisol stopped in front of Jeffrey and faced him with a proud smile and sparkling eyes. For a long moment, neither one spoke, then Marisol stepped forward and gave him a tight hug.

Jeffrey blushed a deep red. When Marisol released him, he stepped back, fumbling for words. He lowered his face and hurried away.

Marisol and Susie watched as Jeffrey ran back to his house, hurried inside and slammed the door. "Weird," Susie mumbled. "Very weird."

As Jeffrey stepped into his living room, he saw his parents staring at him with concern.

"Jeffrey," his father said, "I just got off the phone with Mike Kozlowski."

Jeffrey froze. His father's look was grim and his mother's eyes were moist.

"Are you mad?" Jeffrey asked.

"Oh, Jeffrey," his mother whimpered.

His father stepped forward and hugged him, and his mother burst into tears.

Back at the party, Pablo was seated at one of the picnic tables, a large crowd gathered around him. Marisol sat next to him and held his hand.

"Sshh! Sshh!" voices called out. "Pablo is going to talk! He's going to tell us what happened!"

Everyone quieted down.

Pablo smiled at Marisol, and then looked up at all the happy and expectant faces around him. He took a deep breath.

"This is what happened," he said.

And he talked for a very long time.

Thank you very much for buying this book! If you liked it, please leave a review on Amazon! If you have a comment for me, or if you would like to join my email list and receive a notice when new books in this series are released, feel free to email me at: mainsmike@yahoo.com

In the meantime, here's a little preview of Book Two in the North Hollywood Detective Club series, available in August 2016.

The Case of the Dead Man's Treasure

A graveyard at midnight is a scary place, and seems even scarier when forced at gunpoint to dig your own grave. With each shovelful of dirt he extracted from the earth, Jeffrey Jones knew he and his friends were one step closer to their deaths.

He shot a look at his best friend, Pablo, digging alongside of him and not betraying an ounce of fear. Crazy, heroic Pablo.... Would his life be snuffed out at age fourteen?

He stole a glance at the two girls, Marisol and Susie, standing at the edge of their makeshift grave. The girls were shivering, less from the cold, biting wind, than from the knowledge that death was imminent.

"That's enough," said the fat man. He waved his gun at the girls. "Get in the hole."

Marisol gasped. Susie began to whimper.

Jeffrey's mind raced. If only he hadn't gotten them all into this mess. It was all his fault. He and Pablo dropped their shovels. The tools hit the earth with a dull thud. The girls stepped into the hole that Jeffrey and Pablo had dug. "You can't kill me," Susie sniveled. "I have a math test tomorrow!"

"Shut up." The fat man fixed Jeffrey with a deadly stare. "You are a fat and clever boy, but now your time is up. Say goodbye to your friends." He laughed and raised his gun....

Books in the North Hollywood Detective Club series:

The Case of the Hollywood Art Heist

The Case of the Dead Man's Treasure (August 2016)
FREE preview at the end of this book!

The Case of the Christmas Counterfeiters (December 2016)

The Case of the Missing Valentine (February 2017)

Cover Design
Melinda W. Burt
Pixel Perfect Publishing
pixelperfectpublishing@gmail.com

ABOUT THE AUTHOR

Mike Mains has worked as an actor, producer and writer in the entertainment industry. In the movie business, Mike developed the ability to read a film's script, and predict, with pinpoint accuracy, how much it would gross in domestic box office. His manual "Why Films Succeed and Why They Fail" is considered an underground classic and the definitive guide for determining a film's box office success.

Today, Mike pens a yearly column for Marc Lawrence's Playbook Football Preview Guide, and specializes in mystery and adventure novels for young readers. He can be reached at mainsmike@yahoo.com

Made in the USA
Middletown, DE
19 November 2021

52913856R10135